PAINT THE TOWN RED

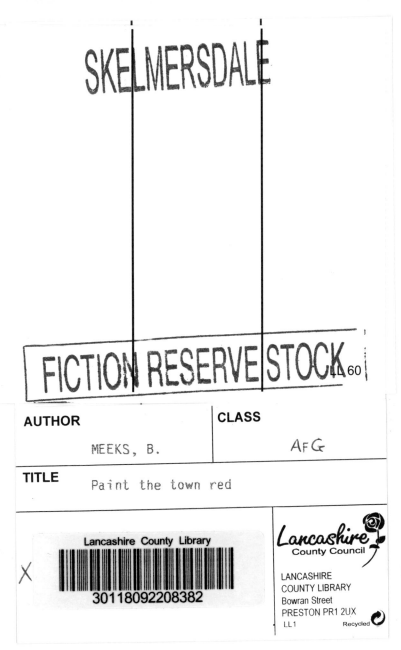

SKELMERSDALE

FICTION RESERVE STOCK LL60

PAINT THE TOWN RED

BRIAN MEEKS

PEEPAL TREE

First published in Great Britain in 2003
Peepal Tree Press Ltd
17 King's Avenue
Leeds LS6 1QS

ISBN 1-900715-74-0

is they who rose early in the morning
watching the moon die in the dawn.
is they who heard the shell blow and the iron clang.
is they who had no voice in the emptiness
in the unbelievable
in the shadowless.
O long is the march of men and long is the life
and wide is the span.

Martin Carter, University of Hunger

ONE: OUT OF HELL

Metal clanged against metal. On any other day it would have been a sickening sound, the finality of heavy-duty riveted iron resonating as a door is firmly shut. Eleven years ago it had been like this, with the late afternoon glare suddenly transformed into fetid gloom.

"Darkness has covered my life
And has changed my days into nights..."

Mikey remembered humming the Marley melody and singing the mournful words to himself. Funny, in times like these is not Burning Spear or D. Brown or even Peter that come to mind; just Bob.

"In dis ya concrete jungle
Where the living is..."

"Oy, Chinee bwoy! Yu tink yu know anyting bout life in dis ya concrete jungle?" Mikey searched the gloom for a face to match this gravelled voice.

"Mek I teach yu de firs lesson. Yu... don'... talk... unless... you... are... spoken... to." With each word the nicked, rosewood baton rose, and in the pauses it fell. Mikey tried to cover his face, but his wrists only chafed, then bled, as sharp-edged steel held them back. He turned to run, but there was only the door. He tried to fall as the ceiling whirled, but six hands held him upright and the sermon continued: "Yu... don't... try... run... when... big... man...

a... speak... to... yu…" the sledgehammer continued, but Mikey was now far away. From a distance – the cold slopes of Blue Mountain Peak, perhaps – he heard words and a hammer striking its anvil: "An... one... ting... yu... dont... bloodclaat... do... is... try... sing... in... my... presence... For... me… nuh... love... Chinee... bwoy... an... me... specially... nuh... love... Chinee... bwoy... weh... sing." It was time for merciful sleep. And so, naked in the cold, he slept. He would need it, some reserve of consciousness told him, for in the morning the nightmare would begin.

Now, eleven years later, the gloom had turned to brilliant sunlight, sharply etching the cars on the far side of the narrow road. To his left, Mikey saw a tight knot of five women huddled in the sparce shade that the twenty-foot wall gave to those waiting for loved ones inside. He turned left to walk past them towards the south end of the street. How little styles had changed. Bright reds and floral patterns. The uneasy fall of bargain satin and artificial silk. The smell of cheap perfume, mingled with the sweat of a half-day's journey. The nearest to him, a slim brown girl with an unusually low bottom, turned her back and said, loud enough for Mikey to hear.

"Me neva know dem did keep dem quality breed a man down ya so!"

Her friend, dark ebony with long blond braids and three gold hoops in one ear, placed one foot against the wall, exposing the full length of her thigh beneath the deeply split dress. Mikey paused in mid-stride, his eyes lowering to the vee where dark thigh ended and cheap silk begun. The woman laughed, tossed back her blond extensions, stretched out her hand and grasped his forearm.

"Long time yu nuh see anyting nice so ee?" His arm burnt and tingled at the same time. Eleven years. In his mind, the door clanged shut again. He jumped, startled, and five pairs of eyes jumped with him, watching intently, to see what he would do. Turning sharply, he faced her and placed his hand lightly on her face.

"Yu nice yu know, baby. But if a go wid yu, yu friend dem a go vex. If it was tree a yu, a might a consider all tree. But me cyaa manage five. So hear whaappen... mek it gwaan til a nex time." He stroked her cheek and in one smooth movement turned and continued walking.

There was spontaneous laughter and a third girl said, "Nuh save it too long dough, or it might'n ave no use again!" Mikey smiled and there was an extra bounce in his stride.

At the corner he flagged down and boarded a bus. Inside hell, there was constant information gathering about what was happening in the world, so he knew that the bus company had been divested eight years ago and the familiar Jolly Josephs – the large, British-made vehicles – pulled from the roads. But not even hell had prepared him for this ride. Fifteen freely sweating bodies were already crammed into the Volkswagen bus, designed in some Bavarian studio to hold not more than eight vacationing Germans.

"Small-up oonu self," shouted the conductor. Despite his unbuttoned shirt, multiple gold chains and mirrored sunglasses, Mikey identified him as the conductor because of the numerous two and one dollar bills strung skilfully between the fingers of his left hand. The unoccupied thumb pointed at Mikey and jerked towards the back seat of the bus. "Dem ave space roun de back. Oy, fat lady, small up yu self nuh, man!" Mikey searched for a space that didn't exist between a fat, half-Indian woman and a thin, dark middle-aged man in a white shirt. It was only the desire to leave the area as fast as possible that made him persist. Half his bottom rested on the woman's left thigh, the other half on the right thigh of the man. He was stretched diagonally across the woman, his back and part of his arm resting on her ample breast. At least his face was close to the window, and as the bus drove to the city, he was grateful both for the good view and the relatively fresh air.

Spanish Town: traffic, congested sidewalks and heat rising from the pavement. He thought of the irony that he'd lived in this area for the last eleven years, but if he'd been left in the middle of it, he couldn't have found his way out. He remembered, though, a hot afternoon outside a cemetery in Spanish Town. Fists punched the air, red flags and banners burnt against the background of the cloudless blue sky and the chants were militant. Next day, *The Daily Gleaner* had emblazoned across its front page:

11 GUNMEN VICTIMS LAID TO REST IN SPANISH TOWN
The bodies of eleven people shot dead by terrorist gun-men on July 13 and 14 in the South West St. Andrew constituency were laid to rest yesterday in a mass burial delayed for days at the No. 5 Cemetery, Spanish Town in St. Catherine. Seven of the eleven buried yesterday died in an early morning attack when gunmen kicked down the doors of their tenement apartment on Eighth Street, Greenwich Town and opened fire on them on Sunday, July 13. The other four, reportedly from Jones Town, died in a similar attack by terrorists the following day, Mon-day... The mass burial was first scheduled for Monday, July 28 but had to be postponed when grave diggers were threatened by a gang saying that "No socialist from King-ston shall be buried here..."

DJ music blared from a speaker box in front of a record store. A slim young woman, one arm akimbo, was pointing her finger in the face of an equally slim young man and saying something Mikey could not hear but could easily imagine. His arm resting comfortably on the breast of his fellow passenger, he fought back, but could not prevent the tears. Carl, Rosie, Charlie... Junior. So many lives had been snuffed out. So many webs had been intricately woven only to be casually torn apart. "There are a million stories in the naked city..." – he remembered the opening lines of an old television series – "This is one of them". So many stories. "In dis ya concrete jungle..." Marley offered comfort again, as he always did.

As the bus left behind the last of the factory shells that lined the highway out of the old capital, an ancient Vauxhall Velox saloon pulled alongside in an attempt to get past. It had originally been blue and white. Now, with a crazy patchwork pattern of rust, body-filler and crumpled metal, it looked more like a skilfully camouflaged all-terrain vehicle. Four battered suitcases were on the roof, while inside, only just visible behind the blue fumes that veiled the car, were six well-dressed passengers. On their way to foreign, Mikey thought.

This would have been a very minor moment in an eventful day, but something was nagging. No, he didn't recognize any of the people in the car, nor for that matter, any of the faces on the bus. What was it? It came suddenly. It was the car. Long ago, Daddy had owned a car like that. It was blue and white and two-toned, and the scent of leather made it smell of home. He craned his neck forward to see where the car had gone. It had passed the bus and was now slowly winding its way through the traffic. Soon it would disappear along with its pall of smoke. In a panic, Mikey grasped the edge of the sliding window, put his head into the airstream outside the bus and was about to shout through the traffic to tell the driver of the Vauxhall to stop, when one of his neighbours, the fat, half-Indian woman, punctured his daydream. "But a wha do dis man dough, ee? De bus ovahpack aready an im dis a move bout, move bout so!" Sweating profusely, despite the airstream, Mikey said "Sorry lady" and made himself as small as possible.

11

TWO: ROOTS

It was 1967. Donovan St. Michael Johnson was ten years old. Sitting in the back seat of the new Vauxhall saloon, one hand on his father's shoulder, the other around his mother's neck, his world was perfect. It was seven in the morning, and already the city was only a vague memory as they entered the misty Rio Cobre gorge on the way to the North Coast. Even in August it was remarkably cool as they drove leisurely along the narrow road that followed the course of the green river.

"Mummy, how Sharon love to sleep so much?" Mikey asked, glancing at his seven-year-old sister, stretched out behind him on the back seat.

"You know that is her style, Michael, give her a chance, man." Mikey thought his mother beautiful, and regularly compared her favourably with other women – her friends, pictures in magazines, women on the street. Clarice Johnson was half-black, half-Chinese with a smooth brown complexion and distinctly oriental eyes and wavy hair. In high school, her friends encouraged her to enter the Miss Jamaica competition; with her kind of looks she would be a sure winner. In the school magazine, they voted her most likely to succeed. "With her beauty, brains and vivacious personality, Clarice is certain to go places," proclaimed the short write-up under the picture of the seventeen-year-old girl in prim, white, catholic school uniform. These days,

Clarice would sometimes flick through her old school magazines and photo albums and wonder what she had done with her life. Her father, a Chinese shopkeeper from Clarendon, had married a black woman. Her mother's family, respectable, churchgoing Clarendonian farmers, had never particularly liked "the Chinee man". However, he did provide generous credit, and when Clarice was born he was grudgingly welcomed, if never as a full member of the family. Though not particularly rich, he made enough to send Clarice to Immaculate Conception, one of the best high schools in Kingston, to get the education neither he nor his wife had received.

In Clarendon, Clarice thought herself privileged, but at high school, she discovered that coming from the country she was automatically at the lower end of the social scale. Her occasionally misplaced H's – dropped from "house" and added to "end" – caused hilarious laughter amongst the fair-skinned girls from Seymour Lands and Barbican. But Clarice was bright and learnt quickly. By third form, she had mastered the finer points of the King's English and gained the grudging respect of her classmates by coming fourth. By sixth form, she was close friends with the richest and fairest, and had become the "likeliest to succeed". Then her father died from a heart attack. Thoughts of a university future, slim as they were on his shopkeeper's budget, ended abruptly. With a rapidly shrinking legacy and a terminally ill mother to care for, Clarice could only afford teachers college.

This was when she met Donovan. Don Johnson – or as all his closer acquaintances called him, D. John – had always been considered something of an oddity. The only son of a third generation black, middle-class family, he had underperformed in school. His dad, a senior civil servant, and his mother, a primary school head teacher, constantly berated him.

13

"Look, we don't have money to set you up in business like those other boys at Jamaica College," his father would repeat after each disappointing school report. "If you don't buck up and get the Jamaica Scholarship you might soon be selling dry goods in a Syrian shop on King Street or worse." D. John paid them little attention. Instead of studying algebra and chemistry, he would be engrossed in discussions on the future of Abyssinia, the Russian five-year plan and even the possibility of full independence for the West Indian islands. Among his fellow students at JC he wasn't particularly liked. His radical views were out of line with the motor racing and smoking interests of the sons of merchants and plantation owners. The more generous among them called him "D. John, the philosopher", others simply called him "that damn idiot Johnson" and prophesied that he would end up in a concentration camp like Roger Mais, Richard Hart and other anti-colonial Jamaicans who had opposed British policy during wartime. Yet, when it came to Higher Schools exams, Don came from nowhere to take third place in the island. This didn't give him the scholarship for Oxford, but it gave his father enough incentive to take out a bank loan for him to study at Howard University in Washington.

Howard was a bastion of the Negro middle class but its location in the capital was a good vantage point to observe that Jim Crow was alive and kicking in the United States and Don, from his privileged Jamaican background, learnt what it meant to be black.

There was the time his father had written, asking him to entertain the two daughters of a close friend, on their way to college in New York. The three of them had been out partying and were gliding home on a cloud of bourbon when they came across five drunken southern soldiers. One called the younger sister a nigger whore. The blood rushed into Don's head. He lunged after the skinny, red-faced white boy with a right cross and kick to the groin. In the melee, the two girls escaped, two soldiers were on the ground suffering from concussion and Don's jaw was broken in two places. Fortunately for him, the policeman who arrived on the scene, though white, ignored the soldiers' whining protest that the nigger had started the fight and should be arrested. In later years, whenever Don remembered this incident it rekindled his hatred for injustice and a certain pugilistic pride. He had come out fairly well, given the heavy odds against him.

In 1954, Don returned home with a bachelor's degree in history, unhappy memories of his high school days and the urge to correct all the wrongs of colonial Jamaica. His father, well aware of his son's radicalism and the problems he would face, wrote telling him to stay in the States and train for a stable, sensible profession like medicine, or law. But burning with crusading fervour, he ignored his father and returned the week after completing his degree. Two weeks after landing at Palisadoes airport he met Clarice Chin See.

THREE: BRANCHES

It was a Christmas dance at the Glass Bucket. Clarice had gone with friends. D. John, fresh from the States and bored by Jamaica's slowness, had decided to go at the last minute. The tuxedo-clad bandsmen were playing Nat King Cole's "Unforgettable" – their signature piece of recent months, and appreciated on the party circuit because it sounded exactly like the original. Mutual friends had introduced them. He, tall and handsome, with the unmistakable aura of someone who had lived and studied abroad; she stunning in a pink, strapless, cleavage-revealing dress, surrounded by a tight circle of suitors. If not love at first sight, then it was love after "Unforgettable" – or so they would reminisce to each other in years to come. Their friends, as they watched the couple dance together for the remainder of the night, had no doubt that something had clicked.

Six months later, Donovan and Clarice were married, though even by then the differences that would later undermine their physical attraction had surfaced.

Clarice, from her rural shopkeeping background, was intimately conscious of the meaning of survival. It meant having a good job, saving regularly and building a house and family. Her time at Immaculate Conception had taught her most of all that in Jamaica it meant making the right social contacts. For Donovan, with his sense of tenured civil service security, this was all just petty-bourgeois nonsense. Jamaica needed to change. If this generation didn't do it, they would have to account to their children and grandchildren as to why they failed. Work would come, he told her, while courting on the verandah of his parents' house in Richmond Park, but the most important thing was to be involved in the change. There was a certain seductiveness to his romanticism, though she was never entirely caught.

"You're a dreamer, Donovan Johnson. Don't you know that nothing in this island really changes? The only thing that you can do is change your place in the order of things. And to do that you have to have money – and friends." But Clarice was flattered by this handsome catch recently landed from abroad with his encyclopaedic grasp of world events and sad, professorial air. "And," she confided to her closest friends, "Him move me soul when him kiss!"

D. John, for his part, was flattered that this brown-skinned, silken-haired beauty was attracted to him. The politics was not a problem. None of the other pretty girls were political. And anyway, he would win her to his thinking, make her conscious by the very power of his maleness.

Three years later, Don junior, whom everyone called by his second name, Mikey, was born. He was followed two years after by a sister, Sharon. Don made his concession to the needs of his family and tried to enter the civil service. Though he had the patronage of his highly respected father, the Colonial Office, prompted by the American State Department, was in the grip of mid-fifties Cold War paranoia. Returning students were vetted as potential troublemakers, and he was blacklisted. The Special Branch report, unearthed thirty years later in a graduate student's M.Phil thesis, warned about his "regular attendance at rallies in Washington at which known communists including Paul Robeson and Richard Wright had been the guest speakers".

But the headmaster at Jamaica College – his old maths teacher – had given him a job against the stern advice of the Chairman of the Board of Governors. At first he had done well. Then the complaints began to accumulate. The fourteen year old son of a prominent engineer had gone home and told his mother that he was proud to be Negro and heir to a great and ancient civilization. Another argued with his father that the Iron Curtain was an American, not a Russian device, designed to isolate the valiant Soviet Union. A third, a white fifth former, and the straw that finally broke the camel's back, told his father, the owner of a major plantation, that sugar was a curse and that it was the exploitation of black Jamaican slaves that made the Queen and Britain wealthy.

D. John was summarily dismissed. He became unemployable. By the early sixties, his sexual magnetism had worn thin. Clarice insisted that D. John renounce his views, at least in words. She had asked one of the local businessmen to employ him as a junior manager.

"Look, Mr. Azziz says he will employ you in the store on King Street, but he can't let the other businessmen downtown know that he's employed someone with communistic views." This was the wrong thing to say. Donovan considered his views his only permanent possession. He ignored her pleas.

What kept them together were the children and the death of Don's parents within a year of each other. His mother, an interminable if silent worrier, had long grieved over Don's downfall. She suffered a massive heart attack. His father, lonely and pining for his lifelong companion, passed away quietly in the night. He left a small insurance policy for Donovan and the house in Richmond Park. This, for a time, smoothed over some of the rough edges and temporarily restored D. John's self esteem. Within a year, however, the problems resurfaced. Clarice left her teaching job and took the very junior management position at Azziz's that Donovan had rejected. She was now earning twice her previous salary. The house was in D's name, but everything in it came from Clarice's earnings. Though Mikey and Sharon didn't know it, the trip to the North Coast in '67 was courtesy of Mr. Azziz. He liked Clarice and loaned her his exclusive weekend house in Montego Bay as a special favour. Mikey and Sharon didn't know, though in later life they would say that the signs were obvious, that these two weeks of sun, sand and fun, were the last time they would ever be together as a family.

The Monday after returning from Montego Bay was the first day of high school for Mikey. He kissed his mother goodbye and his dad drove him to the gates of Jamaica College. That afternoon, he returned home full of stories. There were harrowing initiation experiences at the hands of older boys, candle greasing episodes and the names of a few new friends. When he opened the front door, something was wrong. His mother was, unusually, home from work early. Sharon was sobbing. Immediately, Mikey realized that his father's car was missing from its accustomed place in the garage.

"Where's Daddy?" Mikey asked, fearful about what the answer might be.

"Daddy gone!" Sharon sobbed.

"Gone where?"

His mother hugged him to her, his head resting against her belly. "He's left us Mikey, and A don't think he's coming back."

FOUR: JOURNEY

The minibus wheezed along the highway leading into the city. On his left, Mikey could see the sharp bluff of Red Hills rising from the flat plain and merging into the more massive body of the Blue Mountain range to the East. On the top of the ridge, the most prominent of many mansions stood vigil over the city with an enormous cut-stone wall. To his right, and to the south of the mountain, a thick black pall of smoke rose almost vertically. This was the Riverton City dump, where thousands of the most desperate Kingstonians lived and worked. "Work doin what?" he had asked a fellow prisoner once, in genuine amazement at the use of the verb. "Simple," the man told him. "Yu see when de dump pon fire? Yu tink a man light it because im love see flame? No, skip! Dem light de fire fi bun off de plastic an paper so dem can recover de metal an sell it. Yu tink Riverton City man a idiot? No, skip. Dem deh man know ow fi ustle!" Those who lived on the dump hustled scrap metal. Those on the hill hustled lives and life savings. Four miles separated a life of luxury from a life of shit, but it might as well have been four hundred.

The bus now crossed the underpass that divided the highway from the city. The sudden increase in traffic forced the vehicle to a crawl. At first, the Boulevard, with its back-to-back traffic jams, broken-down zinc fences, mechanic and muffler works and partly finished houses, looked the same to Mikey. But something had changed. It was still an ode to anarchy, but eleven years ago every wall, fence and telephone pole had been decorated with posters, slogans and graffiti. "SOCIALISM NOW!", and not far away, "DET TO ALL SOCIALIST", or "CIA OUT" and "CUBANS GO HOME". The most prolific, however, were those indicating where the politico-military zones began or ended, vividly describing what would happen to opponents who dared to enter. It was "PNP ZONE. ALL JLP DEAD", or, alternatively, "JLP ZONE. SOCIALIST ENTER AT YOUR OWN RISK". All these had been painted over and replaced by fading dance posters, or slogans copied from some drug-riven North American ghetto, like "SPIT" or "BLOOD". Disembodied and without meaning, Mikey thought. At least the old slogans had suggested a sense of direction and purpose, misdirected as that purpose may have been. Now the city seemed to be caught up in a bitter game of survival and had lost its keen, if homicidal, taste for a better life through political struggle. Perhaps this was for the better. And yet, despite the brilliance of the afternoon sun, everything looked greyer and bleaker without the strident red, green and black graffiti.

But there was one slogan that had not been painted out. Crossing the bridge over the large concrete expanse of the gully that bisected the Western third of the city, Mikey saw high on the cut-stone wall a neatly stencilled slogan with twenty inch letters and just two words: REVOLUTION NOW. So it has lasted all these years. Immediately he thought of Carl.

FIVE: CARL

Built in the forties as a solid refuge for civil servants and professionals, by the sixties, Richmond Park was gradually losing its respectability. The pressure for housing had pushed the slums right up to its border. And, as some of the houses in the area began to be divided up into rooms and quarters for working-class families, the doctors, lawyers and permanent secretaries fled northward to the surrounding hills. Those who stayed behind, like Clarice Johnson, were those who weren't yet able to pay the mortgage for a new house in Stony Hill or upper Barbican.

At first, unconsciously following D. John's principle not to hire maids, she drove herself to exhaustion, going to work, then coming home to mind house and children. It was the arrival of Maud that helped her to survive. Maud, like Clarice, was in her mid-thirties, though a life of scrubbing floors made her look ten years older. She lived less than four hundred yards away in Maxfield Avenue, part of the slum housing on Richmond Park's border. Every morning Maud came at six thirty. She would dress Mikey and Sharon for school, fix breakfast, clean the house, travel to the market to buy fresh vegetables, come back in time to look after the children when they came from school and prepare dinner for seven p.m. It was Maud who allowed Clarice to once more have a social life. On occasional weekends when

Clarice was invited out to the movies or went dancing with her office friends, Maud would willingly come and babysit.

But one day, after much hesitation, she approached Clarice.

"Miss Clarice... A ave a problem."

"What is it Maud?"

"A ave a son..."

Clarice looked up, surprised.

"Im go to school at Kingston College and im is de same age as Mikey. De problem is dat every day A ave to leave im wid dese people in de yard, an a dont like what appnin to im. De boy used to be well behaved, but dese las days im not lissnin to me."

"De ting A'm askin Miss Clarice, if it might'n be too much burden, is if Carl can come an stay ere after school an go ome wid me in de night?"

Clarice hesitated. If Carl stayed with her this would mean close contact with Mikey and Sharon. They were already picking up bad influences from the area. She had heard Mikey dropping an "h" while talking to the gardener last week. But she needed Maud. She too had taken blows, and her country roots and years with D. John helped shape her reaction. He was, after all, just a boy. Maybe Mikey might turn out to be a good influence on him.

"Okay, Maud, I see your problem and it's alright. But please see to it that when your son is here that he does his work. You know I'm very strict on Mikey and Sharon and a won't accept any distractions."

Maud would have liked to have hugged Clarice, but restricted herself to smiling broadly.

"Tank you ma'am. Yu won regret it."

Mikey was thirteen then and football mad. He played football during lunchtimes at school with a crushed orange juice carton as the ball. After school, he played again before it was time to go home. At home, before homework, he took out his white and black leather ball and played again by himself in the concrete space behind the yard. He was doing this one evening home from school, juggling the ball from his shoulder to his boot, then to his forehead, when a gruff voice challenged him.

"Yu tink yu can keep up ball?"

Mikey, embarrassed that he had not seen the intruder, stopped playing and held the ball in his hand. "Sure," he said nonchalantly, as though he was used to finding a strange boy the colour of dark, burnished mahogany, with an arrogantly handsome face and a cocky tilt to his head sitting on his back stairs.

"I can keep it up for forty bounces."

Carl kissed his teeth. "Forty? Yu jus start keep up ball when yu reach forty! Watch dis." He strode across to Mikey, who now realised that the owner of the deep if inconsistent baritone was also a good four inches taller than his five foot three. Carl took the ball and seemed to throw it away, behind his back, but to Mikey's amazement it landed on the outside of his instep and was then neatly lobbed into the slight cavity where neck met back. Carl then proceeded to roll the ball along his shoulder, in front across his chest and along his leg to settle effortlessly into his instep. Mikey stopped counting when Carl reached one hundred and twenty. He stood gazing with his two hands in his pockets. At sixty and even seventy, his reaction might have been envy. But when Carl breached the hundred barrier without showing any sign of faltering, envy became admiration.

"What you name?" Mikey asked after a long discussion about Skill Cole, Pelé and other local and international football heroes.

"Carl. You name Mikey?"

"Yeah."

"We have to play some more ball tomorrow."

SIX: SCHOOL DAYS

Carl and Mikey became close friends. Each day after school they spent time on the concrete ground at the back of the house. Mikey learnt how to settle the ball on the back of his neck and then slowly roll it across his shoulder and on to his chest. And Carl taught Mikey how to heng the ball – you had to watch its velocity as it fell and, with your knee raised, follow its pace and collect it neatly in the instep. A player who could properly heng a ball, particularly from a great height, could always expect hearty applause from his supporters during the annual inter-schools football competition. Neither of them was old enough to play, but they worshipped the players and practised incessantly for the day they hoped to run on to the field in their schools' colours.

Their regular football debates involved a keen element of competition, for they attended rival schools. Carl had a scholarship to Kingston College. KC, while retaining its reputation as a prestige school, was located in the heart of the city and had greater working class representation in its student body. Jamaica College, at the foot of the Blue Mountains, was still considered, despite a significant influx of scholarship winners, as a school for the wealthy. One day, after the usual scrimmage, Mikey told Carl:

"Boy a bet yu any money JC goin beat KC by at leas four goals dis season!"

"Why yu seh dat?"

"A watch JC practice, an a don care how good yu seh KC is, nobody can beat JC!"

"Yu tink jus because dem JC bwoy ave money dem can play betta ball dan KC?"

"But Carl, dat nuh true man! Some bwoy at JC rich, but plenty bwoy poor as well. An a know dem have plenty boys wid money at KC too. So how you could seh dat?"

Carl did not respond, but seemed to focus for a moment at some point beyond Mikey. He got up and walked into the kitchen. It was only then that Mikey understood what might be bothering his friend. Nothing more was ever said on the topic, but it was clear as day to him that Carl had focused on the gaping division between them.

Yet everyday they grew closer. Mikey hated mathematics with its tedious routines of learnt formulae and disembodied figures. One day, he stood up in algebra class and asked, partly out of exasperation and partly to attract attention, how quadratic equations affected the price of cheese. The teacher had responded by giving Mikey five hundred lines to be written in detention: "Persistent Perversity Provokes the Patient Pedagogue, Producing Particularly Painful Punishment." Carl, however, was a natural mathematician. While Mikey would subtract the figures in his long division homework, column by column, Carl glanced quickly at the overall sum and would come up with an answer that was usually correct. At first Mikey marvelled at this ability, as he had at Carl's ball juggling skills. Later, a certain reciprocity developed in their schoolwork. What Mikey lacked in mathematics he more than made up for in literary subjects. English literature was his favourite. Carl hated writing and told Mikey he felt like a footballer with two left feet when he had to write an essay. It was through Mikey that Carl began to appreciate the art of reading.

One afternoon they sat down with the prescribed GCE

poetry text of classical poems. Mikey's favourite was Tennyson's "Lotus Eaters".

"A never used to like poetry either, yu know, Carl, until this poem. Imagine, dese sailors after roaming all over the world, facing storm, war, everyting dat can happen at sea, suddenly come across dis island. An what an island! Lissen to dis line.

"All round the coast the languid air did swoon,
Breathing like one that hath a weary dream.
Full-faced above the valley stood the moon;
And like a downward smoke, the slender stream
Along the cliff to fall and pause and fall did seem.

"But dat is not all! When dem come off the ship an see all dis beauty, dat was one ting. Little after, dem discover a fruit call de lotos which grow all over the island, an when dem eat it, dem decide dat dis is de life for dem. Why bother go back home where is only strife an war? Dem decide to just live a peaceful life an eat de lotos and other fruits on de island. Lissen to dis line, Carl:

"Surely, surely slumber is more sweet then toil, the shore
Than labour in the deep mid ocean, wind and wave and
oar;
Oh rest ye, brother mariners, we will not wander more.

"To me dat is life! Imagine. No maths, no exam, fruit on the table every day an rivers an sea to swim in all de time!"

Carl was fascinated by the imagery and read the poem again with new eyes. Halfway through, he stopped and looked up at Mikey.

"But a nuttin strange. Dem man smoke ganja! De only ting is dat Lord Tennyson neva wan to use de world ganja or im might a go jail!"

Mikey was shocked. He'd never thought of Tennyson's poem of escape as having anything to do with the mundane Jamaican world of ganja, police and prison. But what Carl said seemed as plausible to him as any other explanation.

"Yu ever smoke ganja before?" he asked Carl conspiratorially.

"Yu mad? No man, my mumma would a kill me! But dem ave some Rasta man live in de yard behin our own, an everyday dem smoke ganja an beat drum."

"So how dem stay when dem smoke it?"

"Well as far as I see, dem jus laugh whole heap, chant 'Selassie-I', play dem music, beat dem drum an nuh trouble nobody. I feel de ganja mek dem see a lotos island in dem ead, an for a little while dem dont have no worries. But de worries dont go way. Dem only tink it gone."

One day, Mikey came home excited and interrupted the usual football ritual.

"Boy, Carl, we have dis new literature teacher, Mr. Cousins, a young guy, mus be jus turn twenty. Yu know what im bring to literature class today? A portable record player. An you know what im play for us? Tek a guess. Rock steady! Mr. Cousins play Hopeton Lewis' new song. Yu know, 'Sounds and Pressure', an im tell us dat is literature too!"

Carl's mouth was wide open. "Yu mean 'Sounds and Pressure' like:

"We gonna put on de pressure
Sounds and Pressure
We gonna keep on comin in
To this dance..."

They sang the chorus together with the appropriate dance movements, picked up from afternoon television dance programmes, then slapped palms and laughed ecstatically. Mikey was the first to recover.

"A feel so good when im play it yu see, man! An when de whole class get up an sing, yu tink im give us detention or lines? Im jus smile an seh 'not so loud.' Mr. Cousins is de bes teacher in de school!"

For the rest of the afternoon little work was done, as they sang snippets of remembered lyrics and danced to the imagined slow, thumping bass line of the new rock steady beat.

SEVEN: FIGHTERS

One Friday after school, Mikey and Carl agreed to meet at
the bus stop in Half Way Tree and take the Spanish Town
bus out to the Ferry River to catch ticky ticky fish. The Ferry
was a polluted stream on the western edge of the city, which
sustained very little life apart from the hardy ticky ticky.
Mikey kept a pair of Siamese fighting fish. He and Carl
would admire the beautiful iridescent blues and red fins of
the male, which were readily displayed by putting a mirror
close to the glass of the fish tank. The normally placid male
would inevitably spread his plumage and viciously attack the
glass. Males had to be separated from all other fish, although
the females lived in peace with each other. Mikey liked his
male fighter. He was like the strong, brooding character
John Wayne always played, whatever the movie. Solitary but
deadly. Walking quietly, but carrying a big stick. Mikey
thought his male fighter was the coolest fish imaginable,
until one day Carl said:

"A bet you fighter cyaa beat a ticky ticky in a fair fight!"

"Yu nuh serious? My fish name fighter yu know, f-i-g-h-
t-e-r!"

"Aright,"

"Nex week a goin bring a ticky ticky an we goin have a
prize fight!"

So said, so done. The following Saturday Carl brought a

small ticky ticky in an old sky juice plastic bag, tied securely at the top. It was a dull brown colour and half the size of the two inch-long fighter. Mikey smiled as Carl emptied the fish into the fighter's tank. They had bet two and sixpence on the fight and Mikey was already planning to go to Saturday matinee on Carl's money.

The fighter immediately bristled and spread its fins, waving them menacingly in a rippling effect as, like a sixteenth century man o war, it made a sidelong pass at the ticky ticky. The smaller fish ignored the fighter and swam in the opposite direction. The fighter would not leave it in peace, but aggressively pursued it to the corner of the tank, where the ticky ticky had no option but to fight back. Very suddenly it attacked the bright and suddenly very exposed plumage of the fighter in a routine, pedestrian, but highly effective fashion. It first ate big pieces of the tail fin and then attacked the dorsal fin as though it had spent its entire life studying how to eat Siamese fighters. The fighter became submissive prey. Mikey quickly scooped the ticky ticky out with a net and returned it to its humble sky juice quarters. The lesson was not lost on either of the gamblers. Pedigree and pretty looks did not count for much. Mikey had lost faith in his expensive fighter. Both agreed that it might be better to keep ticky ticky and at least breed them to try and improve the dull brown colour.

Every Friday for a few weeks after that they went to the Ferry river with net and sky juice bag to catch fish as well as snails and water lilies to clean the tank. It was June and the time between the end of exams and the start of summer holidays. Five ticky ticky were in the bag and it was getting dark.

Walking down the Spanish Town highway to catch the bus, Carl suddenly asked:

"Yu wan come roun my house before yu go home?"

Mikey hesitated. He had never been to Carl's home.

Carl lived on Maxfield Avenue, less than a quarter mile from Richmond Park, but it might as well have been in Timbuktu. No one, certainly not his mother, had ever forbidden Mikey from going to Maxfield, but there was a hidden code that said that it was not a place where he should be. But Carl was his friend. Mikey said, "Yeah man."

They took the Three-Miles bus instead of the usual Half Way Tree bus, leaving them at the corner of Maxfield.

EIGHT: MAXFIELD

The bus screeched to a stop at the corner of Spanish Town Road and Maxfield Avenue. Mikey noted the small shops lining the narrow dirty sidewalks, the brown bundle of rags that startled them as it stirred, revealing a putrid smelling man lying in foetal position in the meagre shadow of a shop. A mangy white dog sniffed at what must have been the man's foot, which kicked at its snout. The dog retreated with a loud yelp. Outside a swinging bar entrance, two grizzled old men sat on stools drinking white rum. Amidst the loud racket, they heard a familiar Country & Western ballad in which the cowboy falls in love with the Mexican girl. Two boys, covered in soot and of indeterminate age, pushed a wooden cart piled precariously with charcoal against the stream of traffic. White rum mingled with stale piss, old perspiration and exhaust fumes.

Then Carl, who was on the outside, suddenly cut across Mikey, pushed open a swinging zinc gate and said, "Dis is it."

Inside the zinc fence, the sound of the traffic was muted. A large black mango tree shaded a dirt yard. Dominating the yard was an old house with a large verandah. Not very different, Mikey observed, from the houses in Richmond Park, except that this one had evidently been divided into separate living quarters, with cardboard partitions cutting the verandah into distinct areas and separate clotheslines with laundry strung between the railings. To the side of the house, where shade was provided by both the mango tree and the verandah, three men sat on makeshift wooden stools facing each other.

One of them, seeing the two boys enter, shouted to Carl, "Oy, yout man Carl! A oo dat come wid yu? Bring im mek we look pon im!"

The two boys walked over to the group. Mikey, with some concern, noticed that all three wore dreadlocks. The one who had called them, a black man with a broad nose and incongruously thin lips, had greying locks down to his shoulders. He was Jah Tony, Carl's cousin. Later, Mikey learnt that he was only in his early thirties. The oldest of the three, to whom everybody appeared to pay deference, was called Prof. He was a deeply tanned brown man with grey eyes and striking white dreadlocks and beard. The third was a young man, perhaps in his late twenties, whose tight curls stood straight up from his head in what seemed to Mikey an alarming manner. His name was Charlie. In his right hand was a chillum pipe. Mikey was mesmerized at the sight of the fabled pipe, which every high school boy had heard of, though few had ever seen. According to *The Gleaner*, ganja and the pipe were the cause of all the mischief, robbery and gun shooting in Kingston. Charlie held the pipe as though it were a prized object, like an oversized fountain pen. Jah Tony was the first to speak.

"A which part yu fin dis Chinee Bwoy, Carl?"

Mikey was taken aback. Although his mother was part Chinese, he had never regarded himself as Chinese, and at JC, his rich brown complexion and curly hair had allowed him to blend into the crowd without any specific identification. Despite his initial fear, he shot back.

"Me a no Chinee man yu know!"

The three men looked at each other and laughed in a patronizing manner. Carl intervened to rescue the situation.

"Dis a me frien Mikey. Im live up Richmond Park. Yu know Miss Clarice, de lady Miss Maud work for? Is ar son."

At the mention of Maud's name there was a noticeable change of atmosphere. Maud was a dragon for her son and all of them knew it. Then Prof, who was in truth a few shades fairer than Mikey, responded:

"Why fore yu a deny yu nation yout man? Yu nuh know in de las days every tribe shall fin a place in Jah Jah kingdom? Nuh fret yout! From yu a Carl frien no one naa trouble yu. Even as a Chineeman!"

Then Charlie, putting the chalice carefully on a table, melodramatically held onto a curl of Mikey's hair and said:

"But im a nuh true true Chinee! Black man pass troo dis ya ead! A Chinee royal fi true!"

There was more laughter and sport. Then, as quickly as the two boys had become the centre of attention, they were dismissed from it.

Prof said, "Oy Bra Charlie, pass de chalice before it out, for dis is de las draw before I an I go back down a Farm. Carl, tek yu bredren an go in de house, for me nuh wan Maud fin yu out ya so mongst Rasta man!"

The two boys headed for the house as Charlie puffed the pipe and Jah Tony intoned in a loud and pious voice: "Give tanks an praise to de mos igh God, Jah…" and all three men, including Charlie, who was exhaling a dense cloud of ganja smoke, chorused:

"Rastafari."

Carl on Mikey

De firs time a meet de yout Mikey… hmmm. A nevah know ow fi tek im. Me mamma was a work fi dis woman, Miss Johnson. After a while she seh when me leave school me mus come stay up ar workplace. When a see Mikey firs, im favah dem Chinee royal bwoy weh go KC an who wan gwaan like seh dem a royalty true dem air likkle taller an dem skin likkle fairer. So me watch im at firs fi see ow im stay. But after a while me check seh im is a cool yout, you know. One a we! Firs ting me notice is dat anyting Mikey ave, im always willin fi share. Anyting! Book, record, lunch money, erb… Nex ting, im always check fi sufferer, you know! Whedder is yout a wash winshield, cripple man, mad man, Mikey always fin a thrupence, even if im don ave it. After dat, me an im turn bredren, you know! Nuttn cyaa part we.

But one ting me definitely ave fi seh! When me firs meet im, im couldn kick ball fi save im life!

NINE: JOURNEY

Dunrobin Avenue. Kingston began to change from zinc fence to privet hedge. The traffic thinned and the air smelled cleaner and felt cooler. Both of Mikey's fellow passengers from Spanish Town disembarked and there was now more room to stretch out and think. Caroline and Rosie. Rosie and Caroline. Like a videotape on continuous loop, these two names flashed repeatedly through his mind. First it was Rosie, then Caroline, then Rosie until it became a blur. What was it about him that constantly bound him to women and they to him? His mother, sister Sharon, Miss Maud loomed larger than life, and in his own way he worshipped them all. His dad towered as the heavenly icon who could do no wrong, but these three were the earthly trinity who translated the gospel and gave life texture and meaning. Clarice set the rules, Maud enforced them and Sharon, little sister though she was, never failed to remind him what was right. Like the time when he was fourteen and had gone into the bathroom to smoke a cigarette butt. Sharon peeped and told Miss Maud the following day, who in turn gave him a beating with an old tennis shoe. But it was his mother's punishment and gating for one month, with a further month without movies at the Carib, that was most painful. Now they were gone. Mom and Sharon were in Miami these past ten years, running from the scars and pain of that year. Miss Maud was in New York. Only Caroline had come to visit him. At first, she would bring Sunday lunch with the usual stewed chicken and rice and peas. What he remembered most was the fried plantain, with its savoury-sweet scent, so alien to the noxious antiseptic-coated piss smell of the prison meeting room. They talked about news, politics and the latest atrocities committed by the government and police. Sometimes Mikey imagined he saw her gazing at him. But when he looked her in the eye, she always turned away, never encouraging talk about them or the days when together they were going to change the world. Then Caroline stopped coming. He missed the lunch. But he missed her presence more. Her just being there was always more important than what was said. But she never came back.

And Rosie could not come, because she was gone.

TEN: ROSIE

Mikey and Carl left the three Rasta men swathed in their bittersweet ganja smoke and walked towards the small aqua and pink concrete block house that occupied most of the dirt yard. On the narrow verandah, two five or six-year-old children, snot freely draining from their nostrils, played with a punctured rubber ball. Carl introduced them as his twin cousins Natasha and Rohan. They were Prof's children. Noticing their big cousin Carl, they immediately forgot their ball game and ran to greet him. Just then a voice from the shadow of the living room shouted:

"Natty and Rohan, why you don leave Carl an im frien an stop min big people business!"

Mikey looked up, startled by the voice, as a young girl, no older than they, now appeared at the door.

Carl said: "Dis is me other cousin, Rosie. Rosie, dis is Mikey."

"Hello Rosie."

Mikey was taken aback. The girl standing at the door was not what he had expected. She had her father's grey eyes, which in her nut-brown complexion could only be described as exotic. She wore a clinging mini-dress that gave a faint, though tantalizing, hint of hips and breasts. Her crinkly reddish-brown hair was cut in a low Afro, framing a face, which his limited dictionary of poetic terms could only define as angelic.

"Hello Mikey."

Rosie gave a coy smile, looked him up and down then turned away, taking the twins inside the house to clean up.

Mikey stood in silence and stared.

"It look like seh you like ar?" Carl said, smiling and jabbing his friend in the side. "Jus min yu don mek Uncle Prof know. Cause im is a fisherman an im seh any man trouble im flower Rosie goin know ow fish feel when spear gun pierce im side!"

Carl laughed again and Mikey was suddenly aware of his fixed grin. This little girl had turned his system upside down.

"Come, it late. Mek we go back up Richmond Park before Miss Maud start notice ow long it tek yu fi come ome."

Mikey pretended that it might have been the smoke from the ganja that had him in a daze on the way home, but both he and Carl knew the real reason. He had been smitten and there was nothing anyone could do about it.

ELEVEN: NORBROOK

At the corner of Dunrobin and Constant Spring Road, Mikey left the smaller vehicle and took a larger "Quarter Million". On the way to Constant Spring he noted how this commercial area had grown, with its conveniently segregated shopping and entertainment plazas for the better-offs. Glitzy neon signs flashed frenetically in boutiques and fast food restaurants. Outside, BMWs and Mercedes Benz competed with shiny Hondas and Volvos for the limited parking spaces. In Constant Spring, where a thriving market was one of the few places that poor and wealthy met to trade fresh produce, he got off the bus and began the walk up the hill to Caroline's house.

In Norbrook little had changed. The large guango trees still shaded the road from the afternoon sun. Huge guard dogs, now supplemented by uniformed though slumbering guards, stood sentinel behind the tall wrought iron gates of veiled mansions. Halfway up the gradual incline of Norbrook Road, he stopped in front of an automatic gate that opened onto a wide, palm-fringed lawn. Behind it, partly obscured by a freely growing bougainvillea plant, was a large but beautifully proportioned shingle-roofed house that hugged the undulating landscape. He saw the buzzer and two-way intercom on the gate and pressed it.

41

"Hello."

A crackly voice answered.

"Hello… Is that Mrs. Barnett? This is Michael Johnson. I came to see Caroline."

The silence lasted long enough for Mikey to press the buzzer twice again without any response. Then, when he had just given up, the front door opened and a slight, dark figure walked out and came to the gate. Mikey recognized the blue-grey hair and haughty bearing of Caroline's mother, Mrs. Jeanette Barnett, QC. She stared at him with a mixture of wonder and sadness.

"Mikey, what yu doing here? Them let you out of prison? You don't think you cause enough problems already? What you want to see Caroline for?"

She shot out the questions as though addressing a hostile witness. Yet Mikey knew that Mrs. Barnett, unlike her volatile husband, had always had a soft spot for him.

"Yes, Mrs. B. Only this morning them let me out. But you know I was never guilty. Is a frame up! Is Caroline here? Do, please, A mus see her."

Mrs. Barnett averted her eyes and stared at the ground for a long time.

"What's the matter, Mrs. B? Nothing don happen to Caroline?"

"Mikey, Mikey. Yu get yuself involve in all kinds of wrong doing. Yu go to jail for ten years. Yu come out now an ex-convict. What yu expect to happen. Yu didn't hear the news? Caroline is married."

The news hit him like the pressure from the first note of an eighteen-inch bass speaker in a dance hall, though he had long suspected that this was what had happened and why Caroline had stopped coming to visit him. As if from a distance, he heard himself asking: "So, where does she live now?"

"But you can't expect me to tell you that, Mikey? What

would I tell the young people if you were to turn up on their verandah and go and disturb their business?"

There was a pleading tone behind the harsh formality of her voice, but Mikey knew that he was not going to get very far with his request.

"You know my advice to you, Michael? Try yu best an leave this country. Yu mother an sister are in Miami. Yu father is God only knows where. Yu have nobody here, and yu just come out of prison. Forget Caroline..."

Just then, she was interrupted by another familiar voice from inside the house.

"Jeanette! Jeanette! Yu out by the gate?... Jeanette!"

Mrs. Barnett looked back furtively and quickly turned to Mikey. "Lord, don't mek Trevor come an fin yu out here! Come boy, leave the place now! Phone me at work and I will try to help yu out. But, Mikey..." She pointed her index finger directly at him. "Forget Caroline an her husband. Goodbye."

Jeanette Barnett turned and was gone. Mikey watched her retreating, and considered for a moment following her into the yard to plead for Caroline's address. Then he thought the better of it when he glimpsed the imposing figure of Dr. Trevor Barnett opening the door and coming to see who his wife had been with at the gate.

He quickly crossed the road and started back down the slope to Constant Spring. Still in a daze, he had no idea what to do next. Then, he heard a half-whistle, half-hissing sound. He started, but at first saw no one. Then, between the clumps of the Barnett's bougainvillea hedge he recognized the slight figure of Caleb.

"Oy, Mikey! Mikey dread! A you dat?"

Caleb, the Barnett's gardener, had been weeding at the far end of the property and hadn't noticed Mikey's arrival. He smiled at the familiar face. Caleb was not much older than he and had worked with the family since he was twelve.

He lived in a small room in the back of the Barnett's house without paying rent. In exchange, he weeded, mowed, was the general handyman and delivery boy and doubled as butler and waiter whenever the Barnetts threw their parties, though these had become less frequent in recent times.

"So whaappen dread! Dem let de I out a ell! Bwoy, me neva tink me would a set me eye pon yu again!"

"Hail bra Caleb! Jus dis mornin me leave Spain Town! But me like ow much time de I come look for I down deh!" Mikey responded in a half reprimand, even as he smiled and knocked fists together with Caleb. The Barnetts were genuinely fond of Caleb, who had remained honest and loyal all these years, though more than once they had wondered how he managed to dress so well for the Saturday night dances on the meagre salary they paid him. They never asked and Caleb had, therefore, no need to explain that the income they gave him was only a supplement to his real earnings, which he reaped as the local "house" in Norbrook. Caleb sold little parcels of ganja to all the young aspiring uptown dreads who lived in the community and whose pocket money was sufficiently liquid to buy lunch at school, pay for the cinema at the weekends and provide for a regular spliff in the evenings.

"Cho! nuh gwaan so Mikey!" Caleb smiled, a nervous, ananse smile. "Yu know seh I man always tink bout yu, but me nuh like mix up wid Babylon! Specially dem prison one dem yu know!" he said more self-righteously, stating what he thought would be understood by Mikey as a solid reason.

"A true!" Mikey paused and then said, "But like ow yu nuh see me dis long time, yu ave fi do I an I a favour yu know!"

"Anyting man! Den yu nuh know seh me an yu a bredren from when yu use to move wid Miss Caroline! Come in like yu an me a blood, yu nuh see't?"

"A dat me wan yu elp me wid now!"

44

Caleb suddenly understood the drift of Mikey's request.

"But me cyaa tell yu which part she live, Mikey! Any ow Miss Barnett fin out, she wi kill me! Anyting else man. But nuh ask me dat!"

Mikey paused and stroked his clean-shaven chin.

"So ow yu tink Miss B would a feel if she did know seh all dis time she tink Caleb a simple gardener, Caleb a one big erbs man a use ar yard fi sell erb?"

Caleb's smile slipped, then reasserted itself even more fixedly.

"Cho Mikey! Yu know seh no secret cyaa keep between yu an me! We a bredren from a longa time!"

Then Caleb told all. At first, Caroline had not gone out. She would go to school and come back home and lock herself in her room. Then she had graduated with her law degree and gradually began to see people again. One began to come more frequently. He drove a green BMW, Caleb said. A tall brown man named Richard Garcia with "a whole eap a money". This continued for a year, then quietly, without the big splash Trevor Barnett had planned for his only daughter, they were married and moved to a house on top of Stony Hill.

So she had married Reuben. Of all the people in the world to choose and she chose Garcia. There was silence for a long time. Then Mikey spoke.

"So de I ave any erb?"

"Yeah man, me ave a quarter an couple stick. Ow much yu want?"

"Gimme de quarter."

Mikey gave Caleb forty dollars, and pocketed the quarter pound of ganja wrapped in old newspaper.

"So weh yu a go now, Bra Mikey? Yu naa go look fi ar?"

"You nuh worry bout dat."

Mikey turned and set off down the hill, though this time with more purpose in his stride.

TWELVE: THE NIGHT

At the foot of Norbrook Road there is a fork. One branch crosses the concrete Constant Spring dry river and leads up to Stony Hill and beyond to the north coast. The other retraced Mikey's route to the City. One led to Caroline and the mystery of a love which had been torn apart and a darker, murkier time when things were not all they appeared to be. The other led to those distant, fleeting moments and perhaps the testimony of those who had survived and might wish to recount the events. In a cold supper shop adjoining the bus stop, he bought fried fish and hard dough bread and a tall ribbed glass of Irish Moss. He enjoyed the sharp, peppery tang of the crisply fried fish against the ice-cold, creamy smoothness of the drink. Hot and cold. Crisp and smooth. Uptown and downtown. Mikey thought through his choices amidst the dense congestion of buyers and sellers, comers and goers, innocents and predators outside the market. The first bus to pull up was a green and white quarter million heading for Half Way Tree and Parade. It was clear to him that he would head downtown to Maxfield Avenue. He boarded the bus.

Inside was less crowded than earlier. The driver was not one of the gold-bedecked avatars of the younger generation, but a greying, dreadlocked, bearded man in his late forties.

On the windshield was a red, green and gold Ethiopian flag with the Lion of Judah emblazoned across it and underneath the slogan "Jah Lives". On the thumping sound system was the familiar steady bass and scratchy off-beat guitar rhythm of a roots reggae that Mikey could never forget:

> I was down in deep meditation
> Singing songs of love
> When Babylon took I away
> And hurt I so bad
> Now I want to go home...

What he remembered was the sodium light and how it made everything bright and naked. We need to douse those lights, he thought.

KAPOW KAPOW... DA DA DA DA... KAPOW KAPOW...

There was hysteria and confusion. A small baby was crying. An unseen woman screamed out, "Lord God Jehovah Christ!"

Glass shattered then tinkled to the ground.

KAPOW KAPOW...

We must douse those lights, Mikey thought again, but remained frozen on the concrete. His arms provided flimsy cover for his head. Only one man was calm. Carl was not sweating. Rolling from his stomach on to his left side, he drew the automatic pistol concealed under his blue denim shirt, aimed at the sodium light on the street and with one shot returned the yard to deep shadow. Then he was rolling on the ground through a cloud of dust. What happened next was vague. Later, there was light again and sirens. But something happened before that. What was it? All that came through the dust and the glare was the steady bass rhythm and the chorus from down the road:

I was down in deep meditation
Singing songs of love
When Babylon took I away
And hurt I so bad
Now I want to go home....

In Half Way Tree, he changed buses again and was soon on the way to Maxfield Avenue where, perhaps, these and other answers still lay in the deeper shadows beyond the sodium lights.

THIRTEEN: DREADBLOCK

In 1975, both Mikey and Carl got their A levels and were accepted at the Mona campus of UWI. Mikey did exceptionally well in history, economics and literature, gaining a special University scholarship to the delight of his mother and Sharon. Clarice thanked God at church that Sunday for having brought her son through the trials of Jamaican adolescence without a father. So many of her friends' children had started to smoke ganja and become Rastafarians, like Joanne Douglas, who had gone to Sunday school with Mikey and whom Clarice had secretly fancied as a suitable girlfriend for him. She had left home to live with the Rastas in the hills, causing consternation in her family. Lately, Mikey had started to read some of his father's yellowing books. He had been especially struck by Richard Wright's *Native Son*, and moved by Bigger Thomas' homicidal rage, as a black man in the deep South. Both he and Carl had grown fashionable Afro hairstyles. Carl's Afro neatly framed his face with tight, kinky hair, but Mikey's, with its less drastic spirals, was huge and unruly. It was the cause of many an ignored complaint from his mother and more than one letter of reprimand from the headmaster at JC. But through it all, he had kept to his books.

Carl had not done as well. Starting sixth form as a chemistry, mathematics and physics student, he had dropped the physics in the first year, deciding to do literature, drawn to it by Mikey's influence. He did well in mathematics, barely passed the literature, and failed the chemistry outright. He gained entry to the Faculty of Natural Sciences on the strength of his maths, but without the benefit of the full scholarship Mikey received. Maud thanked the Lord for the new government's provision of loans for needy students. Without it Carl could not have taken up his place. But even with these difficulties, Maud was ecstatic. Her son Carl at University! He had been the first from her family to go to high school and now he would be the first to go to college and become a doctor. She immediately went to Mr. Bucknell, the owner of a small tailoring shop on Spanish Town Road and ordered a blue wool suit. Her son was not going to look shabby when he walked into the big lecture room with the professor and hundreds of better-off students. Now, when she walked down Maxfield Avenue there was a gleam in her eye and pride in her step. She had single-handedly lifted her boy above the rest, as he in turn would lift her from a life of drudgery when the right time came.

At Mona, Carl and Mikey got adjoining rooms on Block D of Chancellor Hall. Mikey had feared that he would feel out of place in this all-male dorm famed for its adolescent ebullience and macho sportiness, but he found that even tradition-bound Chancellor was in the throes of cultural upheaval. Block D had recently been renamed "Dreadblock" because of the large number of self-anointed Rastas who resided there. Mikey's neighbour was a tall, black dreadlocks from Trench Town, known to all as Ital because of his penchant for cooking saltless fish and meatless boats. His former name was Ivanhoe O'Henry, a white man's name that he had changed to Omawale. Since, however, no one on the block pronounced the latter properly, it was gradually phased out, and Ital stuck. Ital was a self-proclaimed Nyabingi, earnest about both the divinity of Haile Selassie, and the edicts of Leviticus. Single-handedly he convinced the entire block, through a combination of persuasion and fear-of-ridicule to forswear pork. Soon, the entire Hall, bar some recalcitrant ham-eaters who stealthily continued to eat the tainted flesh behind closed doors, was pork free. No one wished to be on the wrong side of a condemnatory chant from a genuine Trench Town Rasta.

Carl's neighbour was a tall, fair-skinned and heavily bearded second-year student named Richard Garcia. Garcia had been a year ahead of Mikey at Jamaica College where he had moved in a very exclusive clique that drove cars to school and played golf on weekends. During his first few weeks at Mona, he had grown a beard and become a black power advocate with black beret and dark glasses. Later, he had joined the Twelve Tribes of Israel, but this only lasted until he accused the leader of trying to take his woman away. In his latest manifestation as a committed Marxist, Richard, who nonetheless kept his Twelve Tribes' name of Reuben, dismissed the Rastas as backward and metaphysical. An impressive library of titles by Marx, Engels, Lenin and obscurer publications by authors with unpronounceable Russian names burgeoned on his shelves.

FOURTEEN: BLASPHEMY

Most evenings, after the day's lectures were over and following the inevitable football scrimmage, which lasted until the ball could no longer be seen, Mikey, Carl, Ital, Reuben and the other denizens of Dreadblock would gather to "run a boat" and reason. One cool evening in late November, the pot was ackee and dumplings and the topic religion. Ital cooked a particularly wicked combination of the two. He grated an entire coconut and extracted the milk through an old wire strainer. A half dozen cooking tomatoes were sliced and added together with ample onions, black pepper and thyme. The crowning glory was a scotch bonnet pepper, which graced the top of the bubbling cauldron like a yellow bauble on a gaudy Christmas tree. Everyone agreed that Ital had outdone himself. Ample helpings of heavy dumplings, Don Drummond's "Far East" pumping scratchily from someone's record changer and the after effects of playing too much ball, had induced a state of general lassitude and goodwill when Ital interjected: "Right now, anyone who naa defen Selassie, naa defen nuttn!"

In the range of Ital's repertoire this was not particularly provocative, but unlike other occasions when there was silence or mumbled consent, this time Reuben said, "Selassie a one imperialis an one tief too! Im tek weh nuff money from de Ethiopian people!"

Silence fell in Mikey's suddenly very cramped room. Even Drummond seemed to pause from his mournful solo to listen. Ital glanced quickly around the room. All had heard these combative words; he would have to respond to preserve his reputation.

"Blasphemy! Blasphemy!" he raged. "Yes! Yes! If yu read yu bible you will see dat in de las days many false prophets shall come and proclaim demselves! But mark I an I words, when His Imperial Majesty, Emperor Haile I Selassie I, Jah, Rastafari revealet imself in all is Glory, all weak eart shall quake and tremble! Watch yu self, Garcia! For I an I naa trow I an I pearl before swine! Read yu bible! Read Revelation Chapter Six Verse Six, where it is said dat de Lion of de Tribe of Judah shall looset de Seals! Yu ave de name Reuben, which is a righteous name, but yu a follow white man teachin!"

Reuben was cool as he responded: "But yu naa seh nuttn new! You jus a quote bible, but check anyone who ever visit Ethiopia an dem will tell yu seh de people live in poverty while Selassie live in a mansion. Selassie a one tief man!"

"De firs time I an I came as a carpenter, umble before the powerful, but never again! Dis time, I an I come as a King!" Ital shot back "Yu wan de King live in a one grass hut! Cho! Yu naa seh nuttn, Garcia!"

This was chanted with derisive humour, as if the logic in the argument was so obvious as to not require a response. But no one laughed and Reuben did respond.

"Yes, but if im was a king, im would a do someting bout de poverty dough!"

For a moment there was no response from Ital who stared fixedly at a point somewhere above Reuben's head. Then he lunged across the length of the narrow room towards him.

"A goin lick a guy ead tonight!"

Garcia, taken by surprise, fell backward, but not quickly

enough to avoid the first glancing blow from Ital's fist. Before the second could land, Carl intervened and separated them at arm's length. Ital, still raging at the heathen, pressed forward and Garcia, blood now up, demanded satisfaction. Carl's intervention called them back to reason.

"A dis always cause black man fi suffer! De firs ting we do is fight gainst one anoder instead of try fin ways fi unite! Stop de war, man! Mek we reason out de argument an come back togeder as one on Dreadblock!"

Tempers cooled. Drummond was still on, but it was the rocking, backward and forward rhythm of "Scrap Iron". Someone found a piece of white bread bag paper and rolled a spliff and it was passed around. Ital and Reuben never saw eye to eye on the question of Selassie, but for the moment the war was over and peace again reigned on Dreadblock.

Later, when everyone else had retired, Mikey and Carl leant on the balcony railings with newly rolled spliffs and contemplated the new moon over Dallas Mountain.

"Bwoy, Carl, me nuh know bout dis Selassie ting yu know! Yeah, de idea of a black God is irie, but all dis bible, bible ting! It come in like Sunday school again me idren! An accordin to Reuben, when yu join Twelve Tribes, dem want yu house, yu money, even yu woman! Cho! It come in like a new Bucky Massa business!"

"An a nuh freedom black people want from ever since?"

"Yeah man."

The spliff burnt itself out, as the crescent moon rose higher over the Mona Valley and they continued their musings into the morning.

Carl on Philosophy

*I an I philosophy? Right now, me a nuh Rastaman. Yeah!
Me definitely check fi Rasta culture and livity, an how
from a longa time dem stan up fi Africa an Black Man an
equal rights an justice. But yu see dis bible, bible, chapter
a day, ism and schism? Cho! Me nuh check fi dat, mi
idren! Yu see I an I? Every Sunday from me eye deh a me
knee, Miss Maud sen me go Sunday School. Some
Sunday mornin when me wake up late, is strickly strap
pon I an I back. Me, personal, naa go back in a dat again!*

*Dreadlock? Yeah! Africa Unite? Yeah! Black dignity?
Yeah! But yu see me right now? I an I a revolutionary.
Still a nuh wan yu feel seh true me seh dat, dat me is a
Marxis. Ow me check it, is dat Marx come in like anoder
churchical runnins again, you know? Listen dem yout like
Reuben an Munroe an dem people deh. Is pure "Marx seh
dis an Marx seh dat" an "cordin to dis law of history an
dat law of economics". Cho! Hear wha me seh. I an I nuh
need no more law. A pure law and isms and schisms keep
down black man from ancient times to now. I an I seh yu
mus vank de law an buil a community base on equal rights
and justice!*

FIFTEEN: POLITRICKS

On another evening in early December, following heavy rainfall that left the football pitch muddy and the air free of dust, Junior Richards was animatedly defending the merits of his old Tivoli Gardens High School football team against the opposing voices from JC, KC, Calabar and elsewhere:

"De reason why Tivoli a de bes team is because de community support it. Any time we play a match, de whole a West Kingston come out an cheer fi de team. An yu know, even our member of parliament Mr. Seaga, never miss a big match yet!"

At the mention of Seaga, Carl, whose Maxfield Avenue community supported the governing PNP, was quick to respond:

"Me no like Tivoliites! Whenever oonu play a match dem mus ave violence! Plus, everyone know seh Tivoli is de cause of all de gunmanship in de West. Me no like Tivoliites!"

This hostility from the peacemaker of a week or so before took Junior by surprise, but before he could respond, Ital, pausing from stirring his stew peas pot, joined in.

"Yeah, Carl true word dat! Firs time dreadlocks use to walk from Back O Wall to Trench Town, from Greenwich Farm troo May Pen Cemetery to downtown. From Tivoli buil up it come in like seh yu cyaa walk in a straight line again. Yu ave fi get visa fi pass troo!"

"Before Tivoli buil up my mada used to live a bush!" Junior said. "Mr. Seaga give ar a concrete apartment, runnin water an light! De reason why oonu nuh like Mr. Seaga is because oonu grudge weh im do fi we! Is grudgeful oonu grudgeful man! Furdermore, PNP is a communist party! Dem wan tek weh everyting we own! Mr. Seaga is de only man who can save us from Cuba and communism!"

Carl and Mikey both countered that their Party was "Democratic Socialist".

"So what wrong wid communism?" Reuben asked. "Yu nuh read yu Bible where it seh dat it is easier for a camel to pass troo de eye of a needle dan a rich man to enter de Kingdom of God? All yu have to do is look pon Cuba. Everyone have a job! All de children go school! An hospital care is free for all! Yu don have no ghetto in Cuba an de people happy because of communism!"

"Cuban livin in slavery! Dem cyaa leave de country when dem want! Look how de oder day some float over on a raft asking for asylum. Gwaan support PNP an Michael Manley an yu might soon cyaa leave Jamaica too!"

Junior was overwhelmed by an uproar of dissenting voices. The Manley government was popular for its policies of free education and public housing. Michael himself, linked to his father Norman, one of the "Founders of the Nation", with his own charismatic personality seemed to embody a new Jamaica, more for the poor and black. With no allies, Junior beat a hasty retreat from the room. He continued for a time to keep goal for the Block and even the Hall, though he was never heard discussing politics in public for the remainder of his truncated university career.

With Junior's departure, the chorus of argumentative voices gradually subsided. Ital served his stewed peas and white rice, without, of course, the traditional pig's tail. Late into the night they discussed the merits of socialism and communism and whether the theories of white men in Germany could have any relevance for the children of slaves in Jamaica. Reuben argued that Marx and Engels had discovered the scientific way to understand history and politics and that science had no colour, was either right or wrong. Most of the others were wary of supporting a white man's philosophy, but couldn't deny the fact that it was Marxism that was guiding the freedom fighters in Angola, Guinea Bissau and Mozambique. And in Vietnam, the Vietcong were giving the Americans a hiding and they were Marxists too. Why had books and literature from Cuba been banned in Jamaica for so long? It was good the ban was lifted by the Manley government. If Castro was so wicked, why not let people hear as much about him as possible so they could see the wickedness for themselves? Even Ital found common cause with Reuben. He appreciated the reference to the camel and the needle's eye and volunteered the example of Jesus throwing the moneylenders out of the temple.

SIXTEEN: WHAT ONE DANCE CAN DO

It was dance night at the Student's Union. Two sounds were competing against each other. Merritone from uptown had powerful amplification and a good selection of rockers, funk and soul music. Stereograph was a downtown sound system that specialized in dub plates – the hardest, most stripped-down versions you could hear nowhere else.

Mikey came down from Chancellor with most of the Dreadblock posse and took up a position in the darkest shadow behind one of Stereograph's ten-foot high speakers. Here, he could observe without being seen; feel the music without being taken apart by its intensity, a fate that befell novices who stood immediately in front of the bank of eighteen inch speakers. He, Junior, Reuben and Ital, differences submerged in the presence of rival hall residents, shared a spliff, sipped Heineken and observed the world.

Even with the full moon, there was little Mikey could see behind his mirrored, welding glasses. He did, however, spot Carl's familiar, lanky silhouette, accompanied by two women. Mikey recognised Denise, a tall, athletic netball player from Mary Seacole Hall whom Carl had been eyeing for the past month. He had obviously built up enough courage to invite her to the dance, though now he was walking a good two feet away from her, as though they had not come together. Mikey smiled. That was Carl all over.

The other girl he did not at first recognize. She was slim, wearing a loose, short dashiki dress. Mikey's interest and memory were simultaneously sparked. He took off the welding glasses just as Carl recognized him and walked over.

"Wha gwaan Mikey! You know Denise. But a sure yu don know dis lady. Remember mi cousin?"

It was Rosie. Four years had passed since he had met and been bowled over by the young girl at Miss Maud's house. She was as beautiful as he remembered her. Her grey eyes, even more striking than he recalled, appeared at once both open and veiled and there was more than the hint of a smile on her lips.

"Yeah man! Whaappen Rosie! Remember a met yu at Miss Maud's house?"

Rosie looked at him with a studied disinterest, then smiled and held out her small, delicate hand. They shook hands, staring at each other for a moment longer than politeness required.

Stereograph's selector was spinning a dub plate version of the Wailers' "Please Don't you Rock My Boat" when Mikey asked Rosie to dance. Without further prompting, she led him to the centre of the dance floor where the crush was greatest. Marley's voice competed only with drum and bass.

Please don't yu rock my boat
Cos I don't want my boat to be rockin

Mikey leaned into Rosie's body and she whispered in his ear, "Yu know, Mikey, is long time a like yu!"

Mikey felt hot and then cold. His response, he thought later, was pathetic. He whispered, "Me too."

Marley wailed:

And oh, I like it like this!
And yu know, I like it like this!

Rosie moved her waist to the bass line. Left and right, left and right. Mikey followed, feeling himself grow hard against her firm body. Nothing more was said as they rocked to the beat, with the bass guitar pumping out its steady rhythm.

Rosie's Confession

A never really wan go to the dance yu know. But Carl was goin, an im tell me im never wan carry the new girl by imself. Yu know ow man stay; im seh im bredren would mout im. Well, yu know ow me an my cousin tight! Even before im mention Denise, a decide a was goin with im.

When im firs introduce me to Mikey, a seh, a who dis boy in de weldin glasses a try pop style? After a while a realize seh a Carl mawga frien from up Richmond Park. But even den, a preten me never too know im… yu know ow man stay. Yu cyaa too mek dem know everyting one time.

But a tell yu de truth, from a see im, a like im style. Mikey ave a cool way bout im. No rushy rushy business. Yu know ow some a Carl frien stay. Like dem wan jump pon yu before dem meet yu! Mikey never stay so. Im ask me to dance an never too push push up gains me. To tell yu de truth, is when I start feel de riddim that a grab im waist an pull it in! Bob was playin. After a while a feel a pressure on me stomach an inside me belly feel hot.

A don know what goin come out a dis. Me nuh ave no time fi boyfrien business. Me ave de twins an me father to look after. A mus finish school an mek dem proud a me. But me fraid dis ting. De yout Mikey move me spirit!

SEVENTEEN: OLD HAUNTS

Maxfield Avenue, again. A decade had done nothing to improve its appearance. The traffic was greater and more dogs competed with human derelicts for space on the sidewalks. But it was as Mikey remembered it. The zinc gate – now hanging precariously from one hinge – still marked the entrance to Miss Maud's yard. The old house was still there, though its shabby appearance suggested terminal decay. In the corner, the gnarled mango tree – now larger and denser with darker shadows underneath – still dominated.

Mikey stopped in his tracks. Barely visible in the gloom under the tree was Prof, with his fair skin and grey beard, and with him was his old friend Charlie. But how could it be Carl and Rosie beside him, as it had been so many years before? Mikey stood shocked and transfixed.

Charlie, still dreadlocked, but wearing a baggy, rapper style denim suit, was the first to shout in surprise and happiness.

"But wait! A nuh Mikey dat? Whaappen me bredren?"

He got up and gave Mikey a bear hug:

"De I free! Give tanks me bredren! A long time I an I pray fi dis day! Me know one man weh glad yu come look fi we!"

And he gestured with his chin in Prof's direction.

Mikey embraced Charlie with equal fondness, but his

eyes never left the remaining three members of the group still standing under the mango tree.

But it was not, nor could it be, Carl and Rosie. In the soft shadows he recognised Prof's younger children, the twins Natasha and Rohan, now sixteen years old. Both greeted him warmly and he immediately understood what had unsettled him. While there was no strong facial resemblance between Carl and Rohan, the latter's lankiness and stance was just like his cousin's at the same age.

But what led the tears to well up in Mikey's eyes was Natasha's close resemblance to her older sister. She was darker and her lips were fuller, but the curve of the eyebrow, the high cheekbones and the smile were all Rosie's. She looked at him quizzically.

"Mikey, yu aright?"

"Tasha, pick some lime an mix juice fi Bra Mikey," Prof called out. "Rohan tek dis money, an mek aste buy two Red Stripe over de shop."

It was only then that Mikey saw that the old man was blind. Prof had never visited him in prison, though, through the grapevine of convicts from Maxfield, Waltham and Greenwich Farm and the occasional spliff or breadfruit smuggled through the system, Mikey knew he had not forgotten. His dreadlocks were whiter and his fisherman's weather-creased skin paler than he remembered, but it was the fixed stare, the off-centred angle of the head that alerted Mikey. Prof's story was blunt and brutal.

That night the police and soldiers had beaten him around the face and head until he was senseless. When he finally awoke, bruised and bloostained, all was dark. Work was impossible for a blind Rasta from a socialist zone. It was Miss Maud who saved him. She brought him and the twins to live in the rented apartment in Maxfield, fed them and sent them to school. Even now when she was living in New York, Maud never failed to send two hundred dollars every month and a barrel twice a year, in June and December.

Prof spoke about his sister as if she was a saint and when he mentioned the good grades both Rohan and Natasha were getting at Ardenne High School, Mikey heard the old optimism, but beyond these subjects, Prof sounded like a broken man.

"Nuttn naa appen in Jamaica. De yout dem nuh wan change nuttn! Yu should ear dem! A pure badman-ism an gold chain business. If yu ave a nice watch no bodder wear it roun dem part yu know! Dem will chop off yu hand an tek weh de watch! Dis country mash up! Nuttn' good naa come out a it!"

Mikey stood in muted dismay. Prof had been a rock for all of them.

"Bwoy... yu know seh me nuh read it so you know, Bra Prof!" Charlie said, though respectfully. "Yu see Mikey, de problem wid dem yout is, dem no ave no one fi go reason wid or check fi dem! De whole a we fight fi a cause an when we lose, come in like we run fi cover. I an I as a yout did ave nuff man like you Bra Prof. Look pon all Bra Planno, Prince Emmanuel an de odder elders weh use fi show de younger generation certain trut and rights! Dem yout today, all dem ave is America! An gun, an money. So dem try go America an if dem cyaa go, dem use de gun fi get de money! Dem ave some good yout out deh, but dem lack guidance. A so me seet!"

Charlie had left Jamaica in 1981, just after Marley's funeral, to do farm work in Florida, but before the contract was over, he jumped fence and shipped out to New York. In the dense immigrant networks of Brooklyn, the Immigration and Naturalization Service could not even begin to look for a missing farm worker from Greenwich. With his knowledge of urban military tactics, Charlie had set up the Steppers Posse, with members from Farm, Payne Lands and Waltham. Steppers carried out many bank robberies in Long Island, downtown Manhattan and Brooklyn; none, he pointed out proudly, with any casualties on either side. Then, after five years of secrecy and high living, the police finally caught up with him in the most stupid way, arrested on the charge of driving with an expired licence. His name was entered into the highway patrolman's computer and within two weeks Charlie, courtesy of the INS, was on a plane headed for Jamaica.

"But is one ting I an I learn in de States," Charlie noted gravely, "yu mek plenty money fi yu self an yu can buy Mercedes Benz an Rolex watch. But after yu ave one cyar an alf dozen watch what yu goin buy? Anodder half dozen watch! Dat naa elp black people! An no bodder tink seh America a nuh eaven! When yu deh a Brooklyn dem ave more ungry pickney, more druggis and prostitute dan inna Kingston! Yu see me now! Me nuh feel good widdin I an I self unless me can do someting fi elp I an I black people, yu nuh seen?"

Charlie had not squandered his money. There were laundered savings deposits in Citibank, Chase Manhattan and elsewhere. With these, he was building a home in Red Hills in which he, Prof, the twins and whichever woman would have him, would live. He had also paid down on a piece of land on Lyndhurst Avenue on which he planned to build a basic school.

"I an I learn from de Black Muslim," Charlie continued. "You see me now, I an I a Rasta! I an I worship Selassie-I! But dem Muslim overstan dat unless black man control im own business, den im don ave no future!"

Rohan came back with the Red Stripes, Prof built a spliff and the three men sipped beer, shared the quarter ounce and reasoned deep into the night about Jamaica, black people and those days and nights long ago, when life was crucial.

EIGHTEEN: SUNDAY

Mikey woke up elated that rainy Sunday morning. He had danced with Rosie until three in the morning, until Carl had tapped him on the shoulder and gently reminded him that Rosie's father was his uncle Prof. If she was not back at home before morning, both Carl and Mikey would have to pay. Reluctantly, Mikey told her goodbye, but not before making arrangements to meet that afternoon in the Chapel gardens on campus.

He was there half an hour early, but Rosie was forty minutes late. On Sunday, the buses were even less frequent than usual. She was dressed in a blue mini dress with a slim black belt in the waist. They sat on the side of the lily pond, held hands and kissed for the first time. Mikey talked about life and ideas. He respected her father and Rasta generally, but didn't have the faith or discipline to be a Rastafarian. What Manley was doing for the country was good, but could he be trusted? He was a well-off, brown man, after all. Black power made a lot of sense but most black power supporters on campus seemed to be posers, whose main commitment to the cause stopped at dashiki, afro and dark glasses.

Rosie agreed. "Yu see Mikey, me father is a fisherman from Greenwich Farm. A don't even have a mother, though Miss Maud is more than a mother to me. What a mus do is pass me engineering diploma at CAST, go UWI in Trinidad

66

and finish me degree. Then a can help me father an me brother and sister. An with that a can help the country too. A support Black Power an Michael, but de bes way I can support them, is to become an engineer."

Mikey said, "Seen," but his mind was more on the fact that her drive and will to succeed made her even more desirable than on anything she said. He kissed her on the lips and his tongue slowly entered her mouth. Her hands played in the thick, curly hair at the back of his neck while his right hand moved past the smoothness at the top of her thighs to the moisture within. He took off his shirt and placed it on the soft damp grass, and as the dusk rapidly settled into night, they made love for the first time near the lily pond in the shadow of the Chapel.

NINETEEN: FARM

At seven, Rosie got up and straightened her crumpled dress.

"Mikey, Mikey, A have to get home! Quick, before Daddy get suspicious! Come, wake up!"

From far away, Mikey gradually returned and put on his shirt, damp from the gathering dew. The trip to Greenwich Farm was quicker than expected. Traffic was sparse that Sunday night and they were lucky to catch one of the last buses to the terminus at Three Miles.

Prof had recently moved from the dirt-poor fisherman's community of Bottom Farm to Top Farm, in order to improve the atmosphere for his three children. His home was half of a small, rented, concrete, Government-built house with a wrought iron gate backed by zinc sheeting.

Rosie pushed the gate bravely, but Mikey, not knowing what reception to expect, lagged behind. When he entered, Prof, his friend Charlie and two other dreadlocks were on the verandah reasoning. Prof's question as to why Rosie was coming home so late on a Sunday night was cut short in mid-sentence when Mikey appeared. Thick silence followed, as Charlie and the two others looked first at Mikey and then at Prof. Rosie he told to go inside and help the twins iron their clothes for school the next day. Mikey was told to sit down.

"Yu see Rosie? Is my bigges dawta dat. Is de flower of I an I garden. If yu eva so much as bloodclaat mek ar pregnant before she do what she wan do wid ar life, a will fin yu any part yu wan hide an cut off yu balls! Yu a Carl frien. Yu a nice yout! Me like you. So dont fuck! Overstan?"

Mikey understood it well and wondered if he would have slept with Rosie had he got this message the day before. He now knew the consequences, but his heart told him there was nothing he could do about it. He nodded quickly and with this, the tension cleared.

Then the other men rose and walked around to the small shed at the back of Prof's yard. There, in a circle of chairs and low benches, were three akette drums, painted in broad bands of red, green and gold. Charlie kept the steady dup-dup rhythm on the fundi drum, Bongo Johnny beat the huge, three foot wide bass drum with a soft and spiritual fervour, damping its boom on every third beat and Ras Joseph, fingers caressing the taut skin of the repeater, played a staccato improvisation that resonated far beyond the confines of the shed.

Prof lit a chalice and began telling Mikey about his life. There was an unknown white father – a sailor – who had passed through the port and left his teenage mother-to-be with a belly. There was a childhood of ridicule when children called him German and teased him relentlessly about his paleness and the father whose name he didn't know. He had stowed away on a ship at the age of sixteen and had many adventures in Panama, Costa Rica and New York. There had been Garveyites and communists, whiskey and rum smuggling; wars in the port of New York between blacks and whites and between American blacks and West Indians. There was Rosie's mother – of Jamaican parents but born in the States – whom he had met in the Bronx and loved, but who left him after the twins were born with no explanation and no forwarding address. There was hardship in New York as an illegal alien. But all through this there was Rastafari, because Prof had met Claudius Henry in the Bronx who had told him about Selassie and read Revelation to him. After this it was clear for all to see. Then there was the vision in which Marcus Garvey himself appeared in silken robes and plumed hat and told Prof to return to Jamaica, "For therein lieth thine salvation." So with a twelve-year-old daughter, twin infants, and bountiful faith in Jah, Prof followed prophecy and returned to the ghetto.

Mikey sipped the chalice and felt himself lifted by the steady rhythm of the akette, the hypnotic tone of the odyssey and the chanting to Rastafari. But could he have faith? Even in this moment of epiphany, he doubted himself.

Prof's Reasoning

Yu ave nuff yout nowadays seh dem a Rastaman. But dem don know de fullness of Jah. Rasta was ere before creation! Mos man tek African fi idiot. Troo dem nuh buil whole eap a skyscraper. But de African was de firs man. An still de African is de only man who fully overstan Rasta. For widdin I an I dwellet creation. An creation livet troo I an I.

No scientis ever mek a man yet! Dem can tear down de fores an mek atom bomb an pollute de water. But is only I an I can mek I an I. Jah dwellet widdin I an dat is de mystery babylon still cyaa solve!

But as Rasta livet widdin I, is one ting I an I know. Me naa wait fi nuh pie in de sky salvation. Me a go fight fi it, right ya so.

So mek dem gwaan. Time longer dan rope. Jah shall prevail.

Selassie-I!

TWENTY: DARK DANCE

Saturday night in Greenwich Farm. Mikey had come to visit Rosie and Carl had brought Denise. A rowdy game of dominoes when Prof and Charlie had twice trounced Mikey and Carl with six-love defeats was followed by an impromptu dance. A neighbour, Dizzy G, strung up his notoriously scratchy and unreliable sound system, one box in front of Prof's gate, the other, down the street at his own entrance. At eight, the music started with a badly scratched version of the Wailing Soul's chant against the greedy, "Bredda Gravilicious". By nine, despite the skipping needle, more than fifty people had gathered. The sodium lamp shone with an eerie glow, leaving few shadows for new lovers to hide in. Carl and Denise slipped out of the crowd and found refuge in the old shed at the back of the house. Mikey and Rosie had no such option. This was Prof's territory and his spies were everywhere. Mikey felt the injustice keenly when he saw Carl slip away and noticed that Prof had given him a wry, encouraging smile. He could only dance close to Rosie as far away in the crowd from Prof as possible.

He felt himself growing hard against Rosie's thigh. She looked up at him and smiled.

"Yu betta tie it down, cause nuttn cyaa gwaan here you know!"

They had grown closer over the months. Rosie was a natural mother to him in ways in which his own had never been. She would cook rice and peas and stewed chicken for Sunday dinner and bring it to him in Hall. She was his friend, sharing his doubts about his own future and the political course of their turbulent country. Their lovemaking got better, though (with Prof's warning still fresh in his mind) practising withdrawal was not much fun, particularly when he was not sure that he had been successful on every occasion. Tonight, with the moon over the pot-holed streets, the crowd of neighbours and friends in festive mood and Rosie's lithe body against his, he felt alive. He felt a completeness he had not known before. He had lost his own father, a figure no one could fully replace, but in Prof he had found a substitute voice of maturity and in Rosie a woman he loved to his heart.

Midnight, and the dance was winding down. Dizzy G put on the Drifters' classic "Up on the Roof" and the small crowd started to drift home. Carl and Denise rejoined the dancers, convincing very few with the attempted illusion that they had never left. Prof was nodding off to sleep on his verandah.

There was at first only one explosion and then a moment's silence. Mikey looked up, startled, to see Dizzy G's lady – a fat and affectionate woman in her mid-thirties – falling to the pavement with a bloody hole in her shoulder. Someone started screaming, though sixteen rapid explosions soon drowned this out. All around people were falling. Mikey pushed Rosie to the asphalt and lay down on top of her. He looked for Carl and saw that he had done the same with Denise. Shoes were scattered all over the Street. Popping gunfire continued to blaze for what seemed a long time. Then there was silence. Mikey started to get up when something told him that he should freeze. A man dressed in full green military-style uniform with a ski mask covering his nose and mouth was standing over Dizzy G's woman.

She was moaning, "Jesus Lawd me saviour, preserve me…"

Mikey couldn't be sure exactly what happened next. It was too fast. In one motion the gun man pointed the muzzle of a long grey and black rifle at her temple and at point blank range pulled the trigger. There was a single loud boom. The moaning stopped. Later, when the police asked him to recount what he had seen, Mikey could only remember one single feature of the man. It was too dark, he told the investigating sergeant, to see the colour of the man's eyes, but all around them, the area that should have been white, looked bloodshot.

Then he was gone. All around him, people were moaning. Unseen babies were screaming. The Drifters still blared scratchily from Dizzy G's set.

On the roof is peaceful as can be
So darling you can spend it all with me.

Carl on Politricks

Yu see me now? Me grow up inna PNP. Miss Maud vote fi Norman before I born. But yu see right now? Me a nuh PNP. Me nuh like none a dem! Election time, dem come roun beggy beggy. Two twos dem gone. Time fi dis bullshit stop. Yu see when me look an see Dizzy G lady pon de groun wid de ole in ar ead? Me mek up me min as a conscious yout seh any man, any man weh give I an I a tool fi lik off dem deh bandicoot ead, any man, me a go tek it an use it. Jah know!

TWENTY-ONE: AWAKENING

Eleven died that night. Along with Dizzy G's woman, three young boys lay bleeding on the street and on the sidewalk. They learnt later that this attack was but the icing on the cake. The loud music had muffled an earlier assault on Eighth Street, where a family of seven had been brutally murdered in their one room shack beside the train lines.

At first, there was only shock and fear. News of atrocities in neighbouring communities mingled with rumours and half-truths. Jones Town – a strong support base in Southern St. Andrew for Manley's Party – had burned to the ground and hundreds of people fled for their lives. The Government old people's home had been burnt down, trapping hundreds of old, infirm people inside. When the firemen tried to douse the flames, they were prevented from entering the compound by withering fire from well-coordinated gunmen.

Two nights later, Prof, Charlie, Jah Tony, Carl, Mikey and Rosie gathered at the Greenwich community centre with some two hundred other residents to talk about the terror. The PNP councillor for the local government division chaired the meeting and spoke first.

"Brothers and sisters, comrades all! Everyone know what appen on Eighth Street and outside Jah Prof house las Sunday Morning. As you know, A'ave spoken with some of you who was dere, an one ting is clear. Everyone oo saw what appen an survive seh dat de gunman dem come down de railway track from de Eas an when dem finish kill, dem get a signal, an dem retreat back to de Eas! Now, I nuh affi tell yu what is to de Eas of Greenwich Town!"

There was a chorused response. "De cemetery!"

"Yes! An me nuh affi tell yu what deh pon de odder side of de cemetery!"

"Tivoli!!"

"Comrades, the labourite look like dem wan kill we out! But mark my word, so long as I, Bernard McIntosh am the Councillor fi Greenwich, nuh more labourite, whedder gunman, politician, nor any kin a tician, nah walk yah so!"

Again, vociferous, tumultuous assent.

"Furdermore, me an de Member of Parliament meet wid de Commissioner of Police, an im promise fi step up patrol in de community an bring de perpetrators to justice. Nuttn more like dis naa appen, comrades!"

But this new assertion brought only a muted, mumbled response. Charlie was the first to talk from the floor.

"Bredda McIntosh, a long time me know yu. Yu come from Farm. Me an yu go first standard and learn fi read same time. Me ave nuff respec! But, me a tell yu straight, me nuh love dem deh police guy!"

This was met with loud cheers from the younger people and nodded support from a few of the older heads. He raised his hand for silence.

"Everyone yah so a PNP! We love Michael an what im a try do fi poor people! But yu see right now, I an I a nuh lamb to de slaughter! If yu cyaa fin de means so dat I an I can defen I an I self gainst de labourite, den, a tell yu de trut, nuh bodder come back ya so!"

There was further rousing applause. McIntosh now looked worried. He had come to rally support for the ruling party and to find a way to address the crisis through the law.

But the meeting had taken an unexpected turn. There was support for the party, but it was far more conditional than it had been only a week ago. Now this thinly veiled call for arms! How could a constitutionally elected government, responsible for keeping the peace, even entertain such a proposal? But he too had seen the bodies on the ground and in the one room apartment by the railroad tracks. Fresh, thick, blood everywhere. Coin-sized pieces of flesh stuck to the walls and flies gathered in droves. That was where his constituents were tonight. It was then that Prof got up to speak.

"Bredda McIntosh, everyone in Farm know Prof as a Rastaman from a longa time. Me nuh wan speak on behalf of Rasta, for every Rasta is a whole, not a alf! So I an I a go speak for I an I self! I an I ave tree pickney. De bigges one stan up in de back a de room. See ar deh. She name Rosie. De odder two is twin. Dem too small fi come a de meetn. Like every fader in dis room, me love I an I pickney. Me a go tell yu one ting. Yu see before any guy come ya so again? Mek sure yu fin de means so I can I can defen I an I children or we a go look fi whomsoever will give we dat means!"

There was a crescendo of applause. McIntosh knew that there was nothing more to be said. He had his mandate. There was one single issue around which his support would either consolidate or whither away. He understood that a corner had been turned. These were no longer his people from whom the party had a safe, overwhelming vote at election time, but a community carving out its own space, if only because their backs were against the wall.

Mikey too had detected a not-so-subtle change in those closest to him. Even as his bredren Carl strove to maintain his trademark coolness, it was evident that he, and a group around him, had provided the loudest support for Charlie's militant intervention. And unexpectedly, right behind Carl, was Rosie.

In the hustle after the meeting, Carl and Charlie slipped out, and returned shortly after. They called Mikey, Rosie and a few others into a corner. Carl had a gallon tin of red paint in one hand and a spray can in the other.

"We goin paint some slogan tonight gainst the violence and the oppressor! Anyone who wan come, jus jump in de car. We goin paint de town red tonight!"

Six of them took to the streets in Jah Tony's battered Morris Oxford taxi. They wove their way through the downtown commercial district, along the industrial belt adjoining Marcus Garvey Boulevard, and back into the city from Six Miles on Washington Boulevard.

At first, the slogans, hurriedly scrawled for fear of being caught, were either directed immediately at the violence, like "NO MORE KILLING!" or more partisan, like "PNP RULE!" But as the night wore on, they became more elaborate, creative and militant. An early version simply said "CIA OUT!" Then someone came up with the clever construction "CIAGA". As the sky over the distant Blue Mountains began to change from deep blue to silvery grey, Carl painted the last slogan high on a gully wall on Washington Boulevard. It was neither partisan nor defensive. In twenty-inch letters, he carefully painted the simple assertion: "REVOLUTION NOW."

Rosie's Conversion

All me ever wan do since a was five is turn engineer. A don know why. Maybe because a never have no mother to tell me bout teachin or nursin or sumpn like that that woman supposed to do. A look on me fada. Poor ting! Im try hard fi look after us! Im sweat out im soul case wid de likkle fishin, likkle hustling, likkle dis an dat. Sometime im gone one week, sometime all a month. If it wasn fi Aunty Maud a don't know who would a min us when im gone.

All me ever wan do is study hard, pass me exam an tek im an me likkle broder an sister out a dis hardship. An maybe buil sumpn, yu know? A house, a road a bridge. Jus sumpn dat serve a purpose, an look good.

But yu see after what appen las Sunday? Bwoy, me nuh know. Dem ave some people in dis country who don wan see poor people prosper. Come in like dem will do anyting. Anyting! Yu mean fi tell me seh, man who ave dem own children, pay some likkle bwoy money, give im gun, fi go kill odder people children? Fi what? So dem can watch people beg dem ten cents troo dem cyar window?

But it naa go so yu know. It naa go so.

TWENTY-TWO: PARTINGS

Dreadblock was never the same after that. The differences had always been there, but suppressed under the camaraderie of block spirit. After the violence in the West, all that was gone. Junior from Tivoli was completely friendless. Before, he'd been only too happy to stay in on weekends and lime with the other brethren. But since the outrage in Farm, he disappeared every weekend and was increasingly absent during class time as well. One Friday, Mikey met Junior, duffel bag in hand, coming down the stairs.

"Whaappen Junior Dread! Look like yu nuh live a Dreadblock again!"

"Yu see right now, Mikey, come in like is a oly war out deh yu know! Yu tink is Tivoli gainst Farm, or Rema gainst Jungle? No, I! Right now is communist a try tek ovah Jamaica! An yu see if dem win! All like yu so, dead, yu know cause yu a miggle class!"

Mikey was outraged. The night in Greenwich Farm was indelibly imprinted in his memory; this anti-communism seemed trite and callous.

"So dat justify a policy fi wipe out poor black people den?"

"Some goin affi dead so some can live, yu no seen?"

Junior slung the duffel bag on his back and slowly walked down the stairs. He never came back to Chancellor.

It was a month before exams. The poui trees had bloomed for the second time, spreading their circular carpet of luminescent yellow flowers on the green turf. This was the legendary final warning at Mona to begin studying, or face the consequences of failure. Carl came to Mikey's room late one Sunday night. He was in a hurry and uncharacteristically agitated.

"Yu see right now, Mikey, yu naa go see me fi de nex mont. If Mamma ask, tell ar me a study ard. Cover fi me, but beg yu, don ask me nuh more question."

Mikey was curious, but knew enough about what was happening in the West to guess what Carl's secrecy implied. But the next comment threw him into turmoil.

"Bwoy, a don know how fi tell yu dis, but de same applies to Rosie. Yu naa go see ar fi a while. But don worry. A will look after ar. Everyting aright, me bredren!"

How could a plan have been made that excluded him? How could Rosie, his love Rosie, be in and he out? But before Mikey could ask these questions, Carl had gone.

TWENTY-THREE: THE CELL

The next day Mikey met Reuben Garcia on the steps outside the library. Garcia's tone was conspiratorial.

"A hear seh yu bredren Carl disappear. An Junior gone too. Yu see right now, Mikey, like a tell you before, what goin on is class warfare! Dis is de start of de national liberation struggle against American Imperialism, an every man have to decide which side of de fence im stan on."

How could a battle fought by poor ghetto dwellers in Tivoli against poor ghetto dwellers in Farm be considered a class war, Mikey wondered, when it seemed that only poor people were dying, and the wealthy and powerful remained untouched.

"Yeah, Mikey, but Marx show you dat life is more complex than it first appears to be. Where you tink the Tivoliites get all dem nice shiny M-16's you tell me you yuself see in Farm? Yu tink dem buy dem wid weekly wages? Someone like you too smart to just smoke herb and talk dis I an I business you know. You should be in the Workers Party if you really wan fight gainst oppression and imperialism!"

Mikey had always looked at Reuben's Marxist group with a combination of humour and derision. It was tiny, it had more than its fair share of uptown misfits who were looking for a comfortable resting-place in Kingston's radicalised atmosphere and it seemed painfully intellectual and disconnected from the life of real people like Prof, Charlie and Miss Maud. But now Carl had gone and so too had Rosie and there seemed a truth in Reuben's words that he had not seen before. That Friday he went to Reuben's cell meeting in neighbouring Irvine Hall.

It was not quite what he had expected. Reuben was chairing the meeting. There were three students from Irvine whom he had seen selling the party's paper at student meetings, there was a Bajan girl from Seacole Hall, a St Lucian who was also an aspiring drummer, a Trinidadian who wore his hair in plaits and two men who worked in the Taylor Hall Cafeteria. And there was Caroline.

He knew her from prep school. She was slim, tall and dark. She wore her hair, against the current fashion for big Afros, almost bald. She came from a wealthy family. Her grandfather had reputedly made his money during Prohibition, smuggling whiskey from Canada, through upstate New York to the Bronx. Her father had converted his legacy into a booming real estate business. His marriage to Jeanette Sampson, a Cambridge-educated lawyer from one of the established black professional families, gave him the respect denied by his bootlegging grandfather's past. Caroline was an only child. She went to ballet, tennis, horseback riding and swimming lessons. At fifteen, she had spent a summer learning French in Switzerland. Even her decision to go to UWI reflected the way her parents indulged her. She had won places at both Wellesley and Vassar, but she insisted that she was going to study in Jamaica.

Reuben chaired the meeting professionally. There was talk of dues, a detailed plan for increasing sales of the party paper and another for recruiting new students on campus into the cell. Mikey was introduced by Reuben as the latest applicant member and was greeted warmly by all, especially the two workers and the Bajan girl who sat closest to him.

The main item on the agenda was a discussion of the theses of the Central Committee of the party. These had previously been circulated to all members except Mikey. Reuben summarized their main points:

"The main thing, comrades, is that the struggle against imperialism is moving to a climax in Jamaica. In other parts of the world it is well advanced. The people have taken power in Vietnam, Angola, Guinea-Bissau, and Mozambique. In our own hemisphere, the valiant Cuban Revolution continues to stand firm and has now been joined by our comrades in sister Grenada and nearby Nicaragua.

"In Jamaica, the Michael Manley Government has been waging an on-again, off-again battle against foreign capital, but the people have paid the price of this inconsistency dearly. In 1976, when the local reactionaries first tried to destabilize the country with violence, the Government called a State of Emergency and locked up the terrorists. The people responded to this show of 'heavy manners' positively, giving the PNP a landslide victory. But since then, Manley has vacillated. He has conceded direction and sovereignty with his concessions to the IMF and he has allowed the terrorists to get away with violence against the people. If he continues at this rate, the people will be demoralized and he will be defeated in the October election, which is now only four months away.

"What we in the Workers Party need to do, is provide the steel in the National Movement against imperialism. Even though we are small, we must act as the vanguard in the fight against terrorism and against the IMF, because we cannot expect the petty bourgeois Manley regime to play the vanguard role of the working class in the historic struggle which is on us!"

These people lived in another world, Mikey thought. On

the street, in Farm and Jungle, August Town and Backbush, the violence was as real as day, but the idea of a world historic struggle about to reach its climax, was, he thought, far from the minds of the people in their daily struggle for survival. But the way in which Reuben had delivered the thesis, in an incisive and businesslike manner, discouraged him from asking any of the many questions that were on his mind.

The other cell members were not so reluctant. The Trinidadian comrade was concerned that there was too little reference to the stage that the struggle had reached in the other Caribbean islands, that there were too many broad generalizations from the Jamaican experience. Both of the workers from Taylor Hall were sceptical about whether the mood of the people was as advanced as the Central Committee seemed to think. Mikey nodded inwardly. But the sharpest intervention came from Caroline Barnett.

"Comrade, my concern is simple," she said in the crisp, nasal tones of the upper middle class. "Even if Manley wins the election, what can he do after? The country is broke. The Soviet Union is completely stretched trying to support Cuba, Ethiopia, Vietnam and all the other poverty-stricken anti-imperialist revolutions. Even if we win, Seaga and his party and all their supporters will still be there. Where will we find the money and resources to run the country and maintain the peace?"

Mikey thought it was a reasonable question, even though it was posed as if the tiny, unelectable Workers Party was part of the Government. He was unprepared for Garcia's response:

"That's a petty-bourgeois comment, comrade! It's precisely that sort of vacillation that has put the Government in the position it's in today! Either we believe in proletarian internationalism and recognize that the Soviet Union has a solemn duty to support sister parties like the Workers Party, or we descend into social democratic revisionism or

Trotskyism. The Soviet Union will come to our assistance, comrade! That is Leninism! Not petty bourgeois vacillation!"

There was no more discussion. Some comrades gave nodded assent to Garcia's retort. Most just stared blankly at a point in the middle of the room. Caroline alone looked Garcia in the eye and Mikey thought he saw her arch an eyebrow and give a wry smile.

After the meeting Mikey wondered if he would ever go to a second. He had never encountered this level of seriousness about organization. He knew that if any struggle was going to be waged, then it would need this kind of commitment, planning and dedication. But would it be a case of swapping black dog for monkey? Who would want to live in a world in which a hundred or even a thousand Reuben Garcias sternly corrected every deviant like himself for "petty bourgeois vacillationism". He was on his way back to Chancellor, thinking these thoughts, when a red Volkswagen pulled up beside him. It was Caroline Barnett.

"Hop in. Let's go and have a drink."

TWENTY-FOUR: CAROLINE

Mikey had expected Caroline to drive to one of the restaurants or small bars that dot the Liguanea area near the campus. Instead she swung the Volkswagen hard right on Barbican Road and headed in the direction of exclusive Norbrook. In Richmond Park, and later when his mother had moved to Constant Spring, Mikey had known comfort. He and Sharon had their own rooms and Miss Maud was there to wait on them hand and foot. But nothing prepared him for the Barnett's house.

At the end of a winding driveway lined with bougainvillea, alamandas and miniature palm trees was a three-car garage. Caroline pressed a remote-control and the centre door went upwards and then retracted into the roof. Inside the house, a large living room with overstuffed sofas and brightly coloured paintings opened onto a broad, covered patio. This in turn led to a pool with varnished wooden deck. It was all tastefully done. The paintings were by Jamaica's best contemporary artists and reflected the colour and the social contradictions of the island, the unemployment and the frenetic jostle of urban life. There was one that featured Rastafarians smoking ganja from an over-exaggerated chalice. Before he was able to fully consider these ironies, Caroline spoke.

"Yu want a beer? Heineken? Red Stripe?"

"Heineken."

"So you a one a dem true, true socialist, who only drink Heineken?"

Caroline couldn't completely break out of her uptown accent even when she spoke Jamaican.

"No man, a jus like de taste."

"Don't give me that! Everyone knows that it's the style in the ghetto to drink Heineken over Red Stripe. But it's so contradictory! At least Red Stripe's local and the profits stay here!"

"Yeah, but is still the same profits. Them don reach poor people!"

"I guess you're right."

She smiled to herself, as though she had made a secret bet that she had won. She opened a bottle of Heineken for him and a Red Stripe for herself, then put on an album by the Congoes. She sat across from him on the tan coloured sofa, one long, shapely leg folded under her.

"You like the Congoes?"

"Yeah, a listen to them sometime... but me favourite is Bob."

"Bob is great, of course, but you must listen to Myton – the guy who's lead falsetto for them. There's something about his voice that's mystical. It won't sell mass market, mark you, but it's the cutting edge."

The long, tense introduction to "Row Fisherman Row" was coming to a conclusion. The drummer was going into a trademark reggae roll to introduce the chorus and Myton began to chant:

Row fisherman row
Keep on rowing your boat
Row Fisherman row, got
Some hungry belly
Pickney deh a shore

Caroline taught Mikey to listen to the song in a new way. It was about fisherman yes, but only on the surface. Below that, it told of an alternative culture of Jamaicans of African descent asserting a world of their own, an alternative community, where sharing and kindness replaced greed and evil.

By his third beer, Mikey was amazed at Caroline's insight into a music and culture he thought he understood. She played the homeric triple album by the Mystic Revelation of Rastafari and he caught her enthusiasm at the merger of the akette drums with avant-garde jazz horns. She explained how in "Bongo man a come" saxophonist Cedric Brooks merged jazz ensemble playing with drums and the New World African tradition of improvisation.

"It's like Harlem meets Kingston somewhere over Lagos, y' know. It's the same message as the Congoes; us Africans staking out our place in the modern world."

She started to tell him about Jamaican art. How Edna Manley, Ralph Campbell and others had started a tradition which was neo-realist in form, but definitely anti-colonial in content. "But Manley's anti-colonialism has its limits, I think. It asserts a basic equality and justice, but does it allow for real autonomy and empowerment? I don't think so."

Mikey looked at Manley's highly stylized charcoal drawing of the "Horse of the Morning", but couldn't make head or tail out of what Caroline was saying. He was trying his best to follow her argument, but four beers and her physical presence distracted him. Even from the opposite end of the sofa, her perfume – woody, bittersweet and subtle – was tantalizing. She wore a simple white T-shirt, which did little to obscure the fact that she wore no bra. Her jeans, cut off at mid thigh and frayed at the ends, displayed dark ebony legs that Mikey thought magnificent..

She caught him glancing just a second too long at her nipples and smiled. She slid halfway down the sofa and held out elegantly manicured fingers.

"What's a matter? Want to see what they really look like?"

Mikey held her fingers lightly and felt a tingle of expectation. He moved to the middle of the sofa and ran his hand up her T-shirt as he kissed her lightly on her lips. But what of Rosie? She was his friend and confidante. She had left to go on a mysterious mission with her cousin. Wasn't that a kind of betrayal? Or was this thought just a way of rationalizing his own imminent betrayal? He still loved Rosie. But Caroline was something else. He wanted her and, right now, nothing was going to stop him from having her.

Mikey was in this state of confusion, hand up her T-shirt, oblivious to everything else, when a car pulled up in the driveway.

Caroline had heard the car and was on her feet getting two more beers from the fridge when a key turned in the kitchen door lock and Dr. and Mrs. Barnett entered the room.

"Caroline, you don't tired play this Rasta music? Lord man, reggae was bad enough, but..."

He stopped in mid sentence as he saw Mikey with his big dishevelled Afro sprawled on his couch.

"Daddy, this is Mikey Johnson, a friend of mine from UWI. He came over to listen to music."

Dr. Barnett made a point of not looking at Mikey as he asked him, "Which Johnson is your father... Keith... Michael?"

"My dad's name is Don Johnson."

Barnett stopped in his tracks and turned and looked directly at Mikey. "As in Don Johnson who went to JC?"

"Yes Sir."

"Well, I hope you have more sense than him. Because if Johnson'd had any common sense, he could have been living in a house like this, instead of God knows where."

He wheeled out of the room, with Caroline shouting an incensed "Daddy!" following right behind.

Jeanette Barnett had entered the room in the middle of

this exchange. She was short and slim and Mikey saw right away where Caroline got her good looks. She walked over to him and shook his hand.

"Hello Michael. I have to apologize for Trevor's outburst. He's been under a lot of pressure lately. The Government's tax people have been examining his books and everywhere he drives the Benz, he's abused as a capitalist. It's becoming unbearable. Yes, he knew your dad and mom. So did I. Yu father was a good man. Idealistic, perhaps and a bit misguided, but a good man. Don't mek Trevor bother you."

She squeezed his hand and Mikey felt an immediate connection. She had reached out to him with an act of kindness, and she had also mentioned his mysterious father. Some day – not now – he would sit down with her and let her tell him what she knew.

Mrs. Barnett went after her husband and daughter, leaving Mikey alone. The last track on the Mystic Revelation album had come to an end and he heard a little more of the muffled conversation beyond the door. He thought he heard Reuben's name, but he couldn't be sure. Then Caroline came back.

"Mikey, I think we'd better go!"

On the way back to Chancellor she talked about her father. He had worked hard for everything they had, hated socialism and communism. He didn't consider Manley a communist, but he was convinced that he was hopelessly, if not criminally, naive. He knew Caroline clowned around with all kinds of leftists on campus, but didn't know the extent of her involvement with the Workers Party. He knew she had been friendly with Richard Garcia and that Garcia claimed to be a communist, but he wasn't too perturbed about that. Garcia's pedigree was too well established for him to ever betray his family. He would grow out of it. When he did, he would be a most suitable match for his one daughter.

"That's why you're the fly in the ointment, Mikey. For some reason that I don't understand, he absolutely hates your father and wants me to have nothing to do with you. Some crazy 'like father, like son' argument, y' know? Well, of course, that only makes you more enticing."

So Garcia had gone round with Caroline. Mikey was impressed by the way she had slipped in this piece of information and also inferred that *they* were already having a relationship. This woman could be dangerous if he wanted any control over his life. But when she kissed him long and hard in the parking lot outside Chancellor, he wasn't sure whether he was coming or going.

Caroline's Claim

It's difficult to say what exactly it is about Mikey. He's not bad looking. A mean he's not matinee idol material! But he's kinda cute in a teddy bearish way. He doesn't have a great body. When yu talking about body then Richard (vain Richard, who lifts weights in the gym three times a week) has him coming and going. He's not even very theoretically astute. I mean, has he even read the Manifesto, much less the Eighteenth Brumaire?

But there's something about him – a style? a stance? those dark, welding glasses? – that just has me a little off balance. Don't get me wrong, yu know, I'm in full control as usual. But he's the first guy I've met who I think might be even a little honest.

Imagine, on our second 'date', he mentions a girlfriend who has gone away for some obscure reason or the other! I hear she's from Maxfield Avenue or somewhere down there... I dunno. Some kind of roots thing he's trying to work out. Anyway, she isn't here and I am. And furthermore, Dad's declared him verboten, because of some ancient high school feud with his father. That seals it. He's mine.

TWENTY-FIVE: SUMMER

The summer was long and hot. More people died in senseless massacres. More houses were burnt to the ground. And not only PNP supporters fell. In Gold Street and other JLP strongholds, other innocents died. Comrades fell and labourites fell. Brother and sister were divided. Even the cemeteries were divided, comrades separated from labourites, but black bodies all. As poor people killed each other in the name of their parties, the cry was that the Government could no longer govern. If it could not keep the peace, whether right or wrong, it had no right to rule. In the midst of all of this, Mikey and Caroline forged a bond.

He had stuck with Garcia's cell because he needed a shelter in the storm. But she was the real reason. He remembered a meeting at Seacole Hall when Reuben, normally so fluent, had stuttered in mid-sentence when he caught them staring at each other. Garcia shot Caroline a withering glance, which she returned with a contemptuous raise of the eyebrow and a half-smile.

That night she came back to his room in Chancellor for the first time. As he closed the door, she noticed his four-foot tall picture of Angela Davis pinned to its back.

"So, yu like Angela?"

"Yeah, I respect her."

"How come you never asked about me and Reuben?"

"Well, yu never said much and it's your business!"

"So, Mr. Michael Johnson, you telling me that all this hanging around me almost every day is purely platonic? You've felt my breast, after all! Yu not interested in whose hand has been there before! Don't give me that bullshit!"

Mikey was in no mood that night for a discussion about Reuben or anyone else. He planted a hard kiss on Caroline's lips and started to unbutton her faded Levi's. When he struggled with a button, she undid the rest for him and then pulled down his pants. In the cramped room, they made love, she sitting on the edge of his cedar desk, her hands squeezing his bottom tightly.

Later, close to midnight, they got in the Volkswagen and drove for four hours across the island to attend the annual Reggae Sunsplash extravaganza in Montego Bay. Bob was on stage, in what was to be his last concert in Jamaica. He was in the middle of "Trench Town Rock" and one of his improvised dances that crossed over from dancehall to pocomania via the Apollo Theatre, dreadlocks flashing everywhere. The bass speakers were alive with pressure and tension. Caroline, standing with her bottom pressed against Mikey, turned around.

"Yu know, Mikey, this moment here in Mo-bay, with Bob up there and us down here. Y'know, it's very special. Will you remember it when you're old and grey?"

Mikey only smiled and squeezed her tighter. His mind was ablaze. He was falling in love with Caroline, but still loved Rosie. If Rosie came tomorrow and called, he would go to her. But Caroline filled a need he never knew existed. She opened his mind in a way Rosie didn't. Their sex was less gentle, more explosive, acting as a counterpoint to their intellectual sharing. The connection with Rosie was softer and more dispersed and lay in the great tenderness that he felt for her. But now there were two women, both strongly felt, and here he was between them.

TWENTY-SIX: FAMILY

One Sunday in August, Mikey visited his mother and sister Sharon in Constant Spring. He hadn't been home in six months. Sharon met him at the door and at first couldn't disguise her happiness.

"Mikey! Mommy! Mommy! Mikey's here!" She hugged him tight, then pulled away and looked hard at him.

"Why you keep away for so long? Mom's been very worried. Every night we hear gunshots and the helicopters been flying over the area. Miss Maud is worried too. She hasn't seen Carl in three months!"

Mikey hugged his sister and smiled. He loved her dearly, but she was hopelessly middle class and wouldn't even begin to understand what was happening out on the streets. "I'm at University, you know, Sharon. It's a lot of work. Carl is also very busy. Tell Miss Maud don't worry. Carl will come an see her soon."

Clarice came in, stopped for a moment and stared at her son from across the room. Then she walked over and hugged him. From her ragged breathing Mikey knew she was crying, even though she never let him see the tears.

Sunday dinner was chicken, rice and peas, macaroni pie and fried plantain. Mikey ate voraciously, making up for the increasingly scarce Dreadblock Ital pots and the more regular, spartan fare of bun and cheese.

Over dinner he learnt that Sharon was about to sit A levels and was expected to do well in all four subjects, that Clarice had recently been promoted in the Azziz company and was now in charge of marketing. But Azziz had always been a staunch Seaga financier, and in the face of what he saw as incipient communism, he had decided to contest the upcoming election as a candidate. He had asked Clarice, as a loyal employee, to contribute to his campaign and she, to his surprise, had refused. He was livid. You were either for or against. Clarice's unwillingness to be roped in had been seen as a sign of betrayal.

"I think I'm going to go to Miami, Mikey. I really can't take this place any more! It's too violent, too paranoid. At least in the States, people couldn't care less who you are. They're too busy chasing the almighty dollar!"

Mikey thought about telling his mother that they did care very much that you were black, but he knew her well enough to know he would never win an argument with her once she was convinced about something. How far he had grown apart from his family! How little they knew about his life or what was happening in the heart of the city! His emotions veered between a detached feeling that he should leave them in their hopeless ignorance and a deep, familial compassion that urged him to tell them the whole truth. While he was contemplating these options, the phone rang. Sharon answered it.

"Mikey, it's for you, some girl named Rosie."

She had come back. Her voice compelled him as it had always done. She was at the house on Maxfield Avenue. She needed to see him. She loved him.

Mikey kissed his mother and sister. At the gate he stopped and stared at them as they turned to close the front grille. They were the closest people to him, yet so far away. Then, he waved goodbye from the gate – something he had never done before.

TWENTY-SEVEN: COUNTER-ATTACK

All that night, Maxfield Avenue was a battle zone. By early evening, buses had stopped running on Spanish Town Road, the main artery that connected and, at the same time, divided all the warring communities. Bus drivers were regularly flagged down and challenged about which side they supported. Neutrality was unacceptable. Drivers were given only one warning to "leave neutral and find a gear!" Owners of red and orange or green minibuses had to pay for hurried paint jobs, because many were stoned and torched on the assumption that the colour of the bus mirrored their owners' political allegiance.

Mikey walked from Half Way Tree, past joint police-army roadblocks, where officers in camouflage and blue denim searched for weapons. In between these there were the community roadblocks. At some, the sentries demanded to know the political allegiance of hapless drivers. In this area, they had to say that they were socialist, or give the clenched-fist power salute. Other freelance roadblocks taxed motorists democratically, without concern for any specific partisan allegiance. Everywhere the familiar orange and black posters of the PNP were plastered over every available flat object.

Mikey had no problem passing the checkpoints at Lower Maxfield, as there were youths who identified him as "Carl bredren", which guaranteed safe passage, with accompanying raised fists and shouts of solidarity.

In contrast to the hubbub on the streets and the bright glare of the sodium lights, Miss Maud's yard was silent and pitch-black. When his eyes began to adjust to the gloom, the first person he saw, standing close to the gate with a broad smile on his face, was Carl.

"Whaappen me bredren! A know seh a would a see yu tonight yu know!"

Mikey smiled and hugged Carl briefly with a masculine pat on the back, masking his deeper relief at seeing him again. He had felt betrayed by Carl's sudden and secretive departure and had seriously considered keeping malice with him over it. But seeing his old friend, all this was gone. And there, in the deeper shadow behind Carl and at first hidden by him, was Rosie. They looked at each other, saying nothing. She reached out with both her hands and held his. Then her head was in his chest and his was on her shoulder and he felt her tears on his shirt and the tears welled up in his eyes.

"A miss you, Mikey. A really sorry bout how things go. A miss you!"

"It's alright; A jus glad to see you."

For a moment it was just the two of them again, like the first day in this very yard, or at the Student's Union or by the Chapel on that wet Sunday afternoon. But so much had happened since then.

Carl told Mikey the news. The PNP had launched its full election campaign with a massive, island-wide mobilization. With the country hobbled by violence and facing a massive flight of capital, Manley was trailing badly in the polls. But there was hope that once the campaign started and Michael went on the road, everything, as in '76, would change. The waiverers would understand that he and the Government were doing their best to help the poor and that it was the IMF and Seaga that lay behind the destabilization of the country. The cause was just, and in the end the people would see. Hadn't Michael himself once said "Trust the masses every time"?

Then, just as things seemed to be turning around, the Deputy Minister of Security was shot and killed in Gordon Town. He had been returning to his constituency from a big rally in Half Way Tree, when he met a group of policemen, Labour Party supporters and the competing Labour candidate from his area. There had been a confrontation. In the melee the police had shot the Junior Minister to death.

PNP people downtown interpreted this as the signal for a general confrontation. Roadblocks sprung up everywhere again. Streets and lanes where hundreds had died in the previous months, prepared at last to fight, or march, or burn, or do whatever the leadership commanded. The killing had happened at seven p.m. By nine p.m., there was still a deafening silence from Party Headquarters, though a rumour had circulated that the order was to cool it. But this, many thought, in light of the circumstances, could only be a false rumour.

Carl, Rosie and Charlie, freshly resurfaced in the community from their mysterious disappearance, decided that there must be a good reason for the silence, but that the crime against the Junior Minister, on the back of all the others, demanded punishment. They would act.

Charlie had, once again, borrowed Jah Tony's Morris Oxford taxi. They were going to look for labourite terrorists and Mikey could stay and it would still be nuff respect, or he could come. Mikey looked at his bredren Carl, his first love Rosie and Charlie, and did not hesitate.

It was a short walk through the snaking, zinc-lined back alleys to Cookhorn Lane where the Morris Oxford was parked. In the trunk, secured by a twist of thick, red electrical wiring, were two M-16 rifles, a .45 automatic and a revolver. Carl gave Mikey the revolver, showing him in one truncated, two-minute lesson how to use it, kept the automatic for himself and gave the rifles to Rosie and Charlie. They drove East on Spanish Town Road, turned right into Greenwich Town and parked a block away from Rosie's house, adjacent to the train tracks. Carl loaded a full magazine into the .45.

"Dem walk Wes fi kill socialis. We a go walk Eas fi kill reactionary!"

They followed the tracks where they ran parallel to the cemetery and then jumped over the wall, moving from tomb to headstone and through the overgrown grass and bush of "Must Pen", the final resting place for many poor people in the city.

There was the painful scratching of macka bush and an overpowering scent of human shit as Mikey contemplated how vast the place really was. When the confrontation came, it was so brief that years later he had to wrack his brain to recall all the details.

They were making their way stealthily through a particularly dense stretch of undergrowth when they heard male voices talking softly. Almost immediately, they saw four men some fifty feet ahead of them. Each had a rifle of indistinct type slung over his shoulder and all were dressed in green military fatigues. Two were bare headed, one wore a black cap and the fourth had a ski mask covering his face. In the faint light of the half moon, Mikey thought for a fleeting second that the gait, the silhouette of one of the bareheaded men looked familiar. Carl was the first to open fire. Then there was a thunderous, deafening, clatter as the M-16s took over. One of the four fell. The others either fell too, or disappeared. There was so much confusion, but by the time the first magazines from the M-16s were emptied, it was clear that there were many more living people in the cemetery that night than they had imagined. There were shouts of fear, or surprise, or both. Then there were returning bursts of machine gun fire. Some were nearer, some further. None came particularly close.

Carl signalled for them to retreat and Mikey noticed how professionally and stealthily Rosie and Charlie followed his command. This time, instead of heading diagonally towards the relatively exposed tracks, they cut a new path through the cemetery in a westward direction towards Greenwich Town.

As they retreated, there was more shouting and the deafening clatter of machine guns intensified. Mikey heard for the first time the unmistakable buzz of a passing bullet – like a supersonic mosquito – he later thought.

Then the gloom of the cemetery was behind them and there were dogs and houses. Back at the Morris Oxford, the weapons were secured in the trunk, though Carl kept the revolver tucked in the back of his pants.

TWENTY-EIGHT: DARKNESS

There was elation and a sense of just retribution. Mikey remembered Dizzy G's woman and the three teenage boys and the helplessness and fear they had felt. Now they walked openly and proudly the short distance from the car to Rosie's house, recounting the brief moment of engagement, as if in the recounting it would become a permanent symbol of resistance. Then Mikey asked Carl about the figure he'd half-recognized in the moonlight. Carl had not seen his face, but as they looked at each other, they both knew it was Junior Richards, the goalkeeper of Dreadblock, their friend and bredren.

Prof was sleeping as Rosie went in the house and brought out three Red Stripe for the men on the verandah. Charlie was still excited and animated, though he was puzzled by Carl's and Mikey's sudden silence. He never had the chance to ask what was bothering them. Roots reggae was blasting from a set in the next road when gunshots cracked out. They had left the rifles in the trunk of the car and the bright sodium glare of the street light exposed them to attackers. They flung themselves to the ground. Only Carl did not panic. Lying on his back, he coolly drew his revolver, aimed and took out the light. But as it went out, it came back on again, or so it seemed. There was a loud clattering like an unbalanced washing machine. A loudspeaker started blaring something Mikey couldn't quite make out. Then a helicopter was above and its light – brighter than daylight – was shining on them. Four, six, a dozen men in blue burst through the zinc gate and through the zinc fence at the back of Prof's drumming shed. They were cursing and shooting at point blank range. The air was thick with cordite. Carl, still lying on his back, was closest to Mikey and swivelled his torso to face the first man who came through the gate. But the M-16 was blazing even as the wrought iron gate caved in violently on its hinges. There was smoke and dust and more rapid explosions. Carl is dead, Mikey thought, though he dared not lift and turn his head to look. Then he saw Rosie leaping over the flimsy wooden verandah railing, making it as far as the side of the house, when there was an enormous jack-hammering of automatic fire coming from the rear, as other blue-suited men burst into the yard. They were on him. He couldn't recall what they said, though they were screaming, cursing all the time. He took a blow to the belly from the butt of an M-16 that winded him so thoroughly that there was, he recalled, no sensation of pain. Then there was a blow to the side of his head and the taste of blood; he thought he heard his name called by a strange electronic voice that sounded far, far away. Then there was nothing.

TWENTY-NINE: REVELATION

At four in the morning, Maxfield was deceptively calm. The last of the minibus drivers had gone home, seeking three hours sleep before resuming the rat race for the early commuters. A few roosters crowed unconvincingly from rusty coops in crowded tenement yards. But within houses and yards, school children were being roused to iron clothes and cook breakfasts. Peanut vendors were roasting peanuts for sale from carts with whistling tin plate warmers. Domestic helpers were awake and bracing for the long commute to the foothills of St. Andrew, to fix the breakfast and iron the clothes of other people's children.

For three tired men the night had not yet ended.

Charlie was holding Prof's well-worn cowhorn chalice in the palm of his hand as they finished the last of Mikey's quarter pound of sensemilla. As the last embers died, the three watched the fading glow as if transfixed, until there was no more light. Then Charlie spoke.

"A ear de elicopter over de soun system, and a loud-speaker like some kin'a instruction... When a realize we neva ave no tool fi defen weself, a jump ova de verandah railin an dive under de ouse. Me go ead firs, an before me coulda draw in me foot, dem start bus shot! But me manage tek time ease in me foot an dem neva see me. A ear de shootin on de verandah, but me couldn see anyting. But me

kinda see when someone run roun de nex side a de ouse…
It was Rosie…"

Charlie's voice broke when he looked up and saw tears in Prof's and Mikey's eyes..

"Me see when dem do it. She neva ave a chance. Dem neva ask no question. Dem neva wait fi no answer! Den me ear when dem start beat someone. Mus be Mikey. An dem tek im weh. Den dem start beat yu, Prof. Somehow, give tanks to Jah Rastafari, dem never even tink fi look unda de ouse! Jah know, if A coulda change tings, a woulda mek dem kill I an I fi mek de yout Carl an Rosie live. But it neva go so!"

Silence fell as jigsaw pieces of memory slotted into place.

"So ow dis helicopter ting go?" Mikey asked. "Ow dem know fi come directly a Prof ouse? No one neva know when we mek de move! No one neva follow we troo de cemetery! Ow dem know?"

After a long pause, Charlie resumed: "Mikey, me neva wan seh nothing bout dis, for me nuh tink it mek much difference eleven years after. But on second tought, yu might as well know. Yu know is what de helicopter loud-speaker seh jus after dem start shoot?"

"No, what?"

"Tek de brown man alive!"

Despite the mellowing effect of the ganja, searing shafts of light went off in Mikey's brain. They evidently knew about Carl's group and planned to execute them. But they had also found out that he was with Carl and someone had insisted, demanded, that he be taken alive. The old law of the island had not been breached. Carl, Rosie, Charlie, Prof were, in the end, all from the ghetto. They were expendable statistics. But he, despite his friendship with them and shared sentiments, was from a different place. Someone had decided to act and someone else had called in a favour. But who was it who had murdered those closest to him? And who had saved his life?

Mikey felt shattered. Even in this moment of solidarity he had been compromised. Charlie saw the embarrassment and guilt that Mikey now felt.

"At firs when Prof an meself reason bout what did appen, bot a we feel cut up. Prof lose im beautiful daughter, de apple of im eye, an im dear nephew. Miss Maud couldn bear it. If it wasn't fi Prof she woulda kill arself. Even dough im get blin, im talk to ar an show ar ow de fada worket in mysterious ways. Den im convince ar fi leave de islan, an set ar up wid some people in de Bronx. But at firs, bot a we feel a way! Ow Mikey get fi live an de odders die."

Then Prof, in cracked, barely audible voice, continued.

"Den when we realize dat dem neva plan fi let yu go, but charge yu fi possession of weapon and ammunition, I an I gradually overstan dat even dough me dawta dead, me nephew dead, yu suffer too. An yu mada tek Carl deat like it was ar own secon son. She neva recover from it, nor from de fact dat ar one son tun prisoner."

For a long time there was silence. The roosters ceased crowing. Minibuses resumed their chaotic competition. Children and workers were on their way to school and work. The first light of morning broke the cloudless, magenta sky over the distant Blue Mountains.

One day had passed since leaving Hell. Mikey now knew that if there were answers to his remaining questions, they would not be found here. He boarded a bus and headed to Constant Spring.

The brilliant morning light filtered green through the sheltering canopy of tall cedar, breadfruit and guango trees. Rain had fallen and the dripping water made a hypnotic counterpoint to the chaotic improvisation of pecharies, pea-doves and woodpeckers. From the upper reaches of Stony Hill Road, Mikey glimpsed the occasional panorama of the blazing City, just a few miles below. Up here was a different world.

He had left the bus in Constant Spring and decided to walk instead of waiting for the packed and irregular country bus. He was sweating freely by the time he came to the narrow marl-covered driveway. There was no gate. The drive dipped into a shadowy ravine and crossed a tiny stream, rising a short distance to a small, white, two-storeyed cottage with a bleached red shingled roof.

There was no sound of traffic from the road here and, in the shade of the trees, crickets and frogs still performed in a raucous orchestra. A dark green BMW 318i convertible was parked in front. Mikey noted with relief the absence of any guard dogs.

He walked up the small flight of stairs beside the car, to what looked like the kitchen door and knocked twice. There was silence. Then Caroline opened the door. She was barefooted and wore a loose-fitting, white caftan. Her head was no longer bald, as Mikey remembered it; long, neat dreadlocks cascaded down to her shoulders. Her face had lost some of the gloss of youth, but that had made her chiselled, Ethiopian features even more beautiful. The mug of coffee she held in her hand crashed to the stone floor when she looked up and saw him and she stumbled backwards.

"My God!"

Mikey didn't speak. They just stood staring at each other for a moment, then, simultaneously moved towards each other and hugged. It was a long, tight hug, full of memory, joy and desperation, of loss and now, of recovery. When it ended, they sat close to each other, in the arch of the kitchen door. She filled a new mug, poured one for him and told her story.

At first life was sheer darkness. The scandal over Mikey's arrest was enormous. But it was a nine-day wonder, soon superseded by the cut and thrust of a vicious election campaign, demonstrations for and against the Government and the daily litany of murders.

When Seaga had swept to power with a huge, unprecedented majority, in his acceptance speech the following day he had vowed to eradicate radicalism once and for all from Jamaica. Everyone was running for cover. The PNP and the Workers Party were in disarray. There were people, on campus and off, who had vociferously supported the struggle, now vociferously distancing themselves from the Left. It had been very lonely. She had thought about suicide. Life had lost its meaning. He had appeared and stolen her heart and then he had been snatched away. Then, the movement itself fell apart.

It was Reuben who stepped in to fill the breach. He had tried to console her about what had happened to Mikey. He had seemed genuine, even though he condemned the act as left wing adventurism. For a long time there had been no hint of sex. Throughout her grieving, Reuben had provided her with both emotional and political solace.

It was like 1905 in Russia, he once said. The first wave of revolution had to collapse for the people to mature. When the second wave came in February 1917 and then the third in October, the workers were prepared and ready to rise up and overthrow both czarism and capitalism. She needed to believe him.

And he was so helpful. Like the night when her VW refused to start outside the library at one in the morning. Fifteen minutes after calling him, he was there with jumper cable and tool kit. As the months dragged on into the first year, Reuben had become a familiar body again, and it was not, she discovered, difficult to readjust to his smell, his touch, and his closeness.

Two years later, to the delight of her father, they were married. He had asked her and there were no other suitors. But did she love him? That she couldn't answer. There was no passion, as with Mikey, but Reuben had been gentle, understanding and most of all, an anchor in the storm.

Then, after she had graduated in law and Reuben in management studies, things changed. At first, her political despair had concerned only the election in Jamaica, but then had come the collapse of the Grenada revolution and the American invasion. This had been Reuben's turning point. After 1983 – one year into their marriage – he had disavowed Marxism and all that it stood for. She had never been certain whether it was the offer of a position on the board of a big conglomerate or a genuine change in ideological perspective. But, like Saul on the road to Damascus, he saw the light and brought the full force of his personality down against the Left, as he had before brought it down against the Right.

The collapse of Grenada and, later, the crumbling of the Socialist Bloc had affected her deeply, but not in the same way. She had always kept a healthy distinction between

Marx and those who practised politics in his name. So when the practitioners failed, it didn't necessarily mean that the theory was bankrupt. She still believed in the people and the possibility of their changing the world, and at first had argued vociferously with Reuben.

But lately there had been fewer arguments, or discussions of any kind. She practised her civil law – mainly divorce cases and the like – and he helped make profits for his conglomerate. They had little time for each other, between the court cases and the board meetings and the trips to Miami and New York to meet with clients. Reuben was, even this weekend, in Miami attending an annual business convention. Life between them had gradually become sterile. She couldn't bear his business friends and their crass materialism. He spent more and more time at cocktail parties and weekend strategy retreats. The sex, tolerable as it had been at first, had diminished and lately disappeared. She was not happy, but there was this beautiful cottage on top of the hill, the comfort of routine, a place to come home to, and the lingering memory that Reuben had been there when she needed someone most.

"And now you turn up, Mikey. Like a ghost."

The tears welled up and then streamed freely from her eyes. He held her, at first gently, and then more urgently. He kissed the tears from her eyelids, her nose and her lips. She returned his kiss, and they embraced as though they wished to undo the lost years. He pulled the caftan over her head and they lay together on the stone floor and made love urgently, their sweat flowing freely, even in the cool morning air.

Later, as they sat on the floor of the wide balcony on the other side of the house, overlooking a richly green ravine, she turned and looked at him in that quizzical, penetrating way he remembered so well.

"The fact that you're here means you've been to see

Mom and she told you about Reuben... So why did you come?"

"I wasn't going to come... A wanted to come... but what was I going to say? Hello, I'm back! Every bone in my body wanted to come, Caroline, but A tried to resist."

"But you're here. So let me ask again. And don't bullshit me, Mikey Johnson, why did you come?"

"Can I ask a question before I answer that?"

"Yes, of course."

Mikey turned and faced her directly.

"What yu know about that night, Caroline?"

"What do you mean?"

"A guess it's my turn to say don't bullshit. Someone knew about Carl and Rosie. Someone held the trigger when it was my turn, but not for them!"

She had put down her mug of coffee and held her face between the palms of both hands. The tears were flowing again.

"I got home from studying that Sunday afternoon... Mommy met me at the door. She was in a state. Daddy and Reuben were in the kitchen talking. She said there was some bad news. Reuben's uncle, a Colonel in the army, told him about this group whom they'd been targeting. They'd been involved in subversion, some gunrunning thing. Most of the names he didn't know. Then yu friend Carl name came up. The plan was to catch them in the act and to eliminate them if necessary. I thought you might be involved with them. I tried to get you on campus to tell you. You'd gone to your mother's home, some guy on the block said. I called her house and your sister answered and said you'd gone down to Maxfield Avenue. I panicked, Mikey, because according to what Reuben said, with all this unrest over the Junior Minister's death, they were planning to act against these guys immediately. I pleaded with Dad to speak with his friends... to do something. At first he said he wasn't interested in helping Don Johnson's son. Then I told him it wasn't for Don Johnson, but for me. He made some calls. Reuben called his uncle. And that was it. The next morning I saw your picture on the front of the *Gleaner*."

For a long time they both stared into the dense foliage as though it was there that the echoes of the past would, at last, be heard and deciphered. But there were no more echoes. She had saved his life, but the price for his freedom had been the death of those closest to him.

"So what do we do now?" she asked, without looking at him. "I've never stopped loving you, Mikey."

"And I will always love you. But you're married to Reuben. I need some time to think."

He held her hand, not able to look her in the face. Then he got up, still holding her fingers until, at his full height, they slipped from his grasp. Then he turned, and without looking back, walked down the marl driveway, down the Stony Hill Road to Constant Spring, and boarded a bus into the heart of the city.

.

ROHAN'S POSTSCRIPT

That was over ten years ago. I left Ardenne with three A levels and went to study film at New York University. Natasha went to UWI to study law. Charlie paid all the fees, pocket money, grocery bills, everything. I didn't come home until I'd finished and submitted my final short film on a Puerto Rican deejay who was more yardie than the yardies themselves.

I'd been back for two weeks, just marking time and feeling the vibe of the city. Tasha, who was practising company law with a small firm, lived in an apartment block on Hope road near Matilda's Corner. I was in Half Way Tree one hot June evening, looking for a taxi to go to Tasha's when, like an apparition from the distant past, I saw him.

From across the road, he seemed to have weathered the years well. His walk was still very seventies, with a sort of careless bounce, like a hungry adolescent lion. He was wearing a faded black T-shirt, matching stovepipe black jeans and a worn pair of tan desert boots – and a black baseball cap with a slim red gold and green stripe dividing the brim in two, and shoulder-length locks. I called out to him and he crossed the road smiling and we embraced on the pavement.

"Rohan, me bredren! Is years and years! Wha gwaan?"

"Wha gwaan, Mikey? Bwaay! Yu nu change much? Mi jus come back from States two weeks ago. Whe yu a do wid yuself?"

But up close it was clear that he had aged. The softness of youth had left him and deep lines were etched across his forehead and on his cheeks, and his locks were generously streaked with silver and grey. We drifted to a bar in Half Way Tree just across the road from the clock and, behind a barricade of empty Red Stripe bottles that grew formidably through the long night, spoke of things and times and Prof and Rosie and Carl and Caroline.

He never saw Caroline again. He meant to come back, but somehow never did. Later, he heard that she had left the island. Reuben still managed the company and kept the house on the hill, but she was never seen there with him, nor on the cocktail circuit.

At first, Mikey had worked with Charlie in setting up the basic school. It had been good to see the youngsters, many of whom had lost parents in the fighting, revive under nourishing care. But things got too hot, with both the DEA and the local cops on Charlie's case. He left for Belize with his wife and son, living comfortably on the interest from his many accounts. But he still looked after Prof, his children and Aunt Maud. Mikey tried to maintain the basic school but it was too dangerous. The word was out that it was built on drug money and the false rumour was spread that drugs were still stashed there. Raid followed raid and in the end he had to close it down. Hard times followed. For a year, he helped a dread named Puppy make akette drums on Spanish Town Road. But in the new digital world there was little market for the red green and gold goatskin drums. Then one day, sitting hungry on a stool on the sidewalk near Tropical Plaza, a silver Benz pulled up beside him. Behind the wheel was a barely recognizable Ital. He had become Ivanhoe O'Henry again, now balding, with distinguished greying at the temples. He had made his money as an insurance broker and promised Mikey a job as a junior salesman in the firm. All Mikey had to do was clean up and drop the "I an I business". Ital/Ivanhoe lent him a suit and offered a room in his apartment until he caught his footing.

Mikey had trimmed and shaved, put on the suit and for two years sold insurance. To his surprise he did reasonably well, selling policies at first to old blockmates from Chancellor Hall. He was even considered for promotion when the entire financial sector came tumbling down. There had been a false bubble of bad loans, inflated interest rates and massive profit-taking that had gripped the country like one big pyramid scheme. Ital/Ivanhoe, Mikey and hundreds of others were summarily laid off. Times were hard again, but Mikey was used to it. Every now and then Charlie would send a little money from Belize via Miami. When my father, Prof, blind and broken in spirit, died of a heart attack last year, there was even a little more money to spread around. Now Mikey was trying to start the basic school again, but this time in the country, in St. Mary, where the air was cleaner.

At three in the morning in the cigarette smoke of the Half Way Tree bar, after Spanish Town, Norbrook, UWI, Greenwich Farm and Maxfield had all been told again, I think, for the first time, I understood the meaning of the deaths of my sister and cousin and what my purpose in all this was meant to be. I promised Mikey that I would write the story and one day, even, make a film out of it. And, though the detail fades with time, I remember his last words as he rose to leave. He said: "Remember Rohan, Marley say, 'Rise up fallen Fighters… He who fights and runs away lives to fight another day.' One day, the heathen back shall be against the wall and I an I shall return." In the neon-flecked dark of the hours before morning, amidst the digital slam

114

of a dance hall rhythm, he loped, hungry lion-style down the sidewalk, crossed Hope Road and slowly faded in the blue haze of the frantic traffic.

Brian Meeks was born in Montreal, Canada of West Indian parents and grew up in Kingston, Jamaica. He has taught political science at the University of the West Indies, Mona for many years and has published three books on radical and revolutionary politics in the Caribbean. The most recent of these is *Narratives of Resistance: Jamaica, Trinidad, the Caribbean* (UWI Press, 2000). He is also joint editor, with Folke Lindahl, of *New Caribbean Thought: a Reader* (UWI Press, 2001).

Meeks's poetry was very much a part of the early Jamaican dub poetry movement of the seventies and is to be found in a number of anthologies, including Kamau Brathwaite's seminal *Savacou ¾*, *The Penguin Book of Caribbean Verse* (1986), *The Anthology of Young Jamaican Poets* (Savacou, 1979) and Kwame Dawes's recent *Wheel and Come Again* (Peepal Tree, 1999).

Paint the Town Red is an extension of Meeks's concern with the theme of rebellion and the existential condition of the Caribbean people.

'Writing *Paint the Town Red* was a cathartic experience,' Meeks suggests. 'There are so many painful, unanswered questions about Jamaica in the seventies, some of which may never be resolved by the historian or social scientist. The normal figure for the number of people killed during the political campaign leading up to the 1980 election is eight hundred, though I suspect that the real figure is significantly greater. Have these men, women and children who died simply been erased from the world, or are there many poignant stories to be told? By locating itself in history while avoiding the limitations imposed by traditional scholarship, *Paint the Town Red* seeks to address, if not answer, some of the persistent questions of that lost decade.'

Geoffrey Philp
Benjamin, My Son

Jason Stewart is in a Miami bar when he sees a newsflash reporting the murder of his politician stepfather, Albert Lumley. With his girlfriend, Nicole, Jason returns to his native Jamaica for the funeral. There the murder is regarded by all as part of the bipartisan warfare which has torn the country apart.

But when Jason meets his old mentor, Papa Legba, the Rastafarian hints at a darker truth. Under the guidance of his locksman Virgil, and redeemed by his love for the Beatrice-like figure of Nicole, Jason enters the several circles of Jamaica's hell. The portrayal of the garrison ghetto area of Standpipe is, in particular, profoundly disturbing.

In his infernal journeyings, Jason encounters both former acquaintances and earlier versions of himself. In the process he confronts conflicting claims on his identity: the Jason shaped by the middle-class colonial traditions of Jamaica College and the Benjamin who was once close to Papa Legba.

Benjamin, My Son combines the excitement of the fast-paced thriller, the literary satisfactions of its intertextual play and the bracing commentary of its portrayal of the sexism, homophobia and moral corruption which have filled the vacuum vacated by the collapse of the nationalist dream.

ISBN: 1-900715-78-3
Pages: 175
Published: 15 May 2003
Price: £8.99

Kwame Dawes
A Place to Hide

A man lies in a newspaper-lined room dreaming an other life. Bob Marley's spirit flew into him at the moment of the singer's death. A woman detaches herself from her perfunctory husband and finds the erotic foreplay she longs for in journeying round the island. A man climbs Blue Mountain Peak to fly and hear the voice of God. Sonia paints her new friend Joan and hopes that this will be the beginning of a sexual adventure.

Dawes's characters are driven by their need for intimate contact with people and with God, and their need to construct personal myths powerful enough to live by. In a host of distinctive and persuasive voices they tell stories that reveal their inner lives and give an incisive portrayal of contemporary Jamaican society that is unsparing in confronting its elements of misogyny and nihilistic violence.

Indeed several stories question how this disorder can be meaningfully told without either sensationalism or despair. For Dawes, the answer is found in the creative energies that lie just the other side of chaos. In particular, in the dub vershan episodes, which intercut the stories, there are intense and moving celebrations of moments of reggae creation in the studio and in performance.

Kwame Dawes has established a growing international reputation as a poet and these are stories that combine a poetic imagination with narrative drive, an acute social awareness and a deep inwardness in the treatment of character. In the penultimate story, 'Marley's Ghost', Dawes's imagination soars to towering myth.

ISBN: 1-900715-48-1
Pages: 312
Published: 01 March 2003
Price: £9.99

Ralph Thompson
View from Mount Diablo

A novel in verse, *View from Mount Diablo* explores the transformation of Jamaica from a sleepy colonial society to a postcolonial nation where political corruption, armed gangs, drug wars, and an avenging police and army have made life hell. Class and racial privilege and the resentments they provoke underscore both the turmoil in the wider society and the relationships at the heart of the narrative between Adam Cole, the dreamy white Jamaican boy who becomes a crusading journalist exposing the hidden godfathers of crime, squint-eyed Nellie Simpson, once the servant who cares for/abuses him, who becomes a political enforcer, and stuttering Nathan the gardener and groom, whose boyhood love for Adam is tested to the full when Adam's journalism threatens to expose his role as a cocaine baron. Beyond this trio is a dazzling array of real and fictive characters including Bustamente, Tony Blake aka 'The Frog', Blaka, an informer who finds religion, a white plantation owner still trying to wield power, and a suicidal police officer.

Louis Simpson, the Jamaican-American Pulitzer Prize-winning poet writes: '*View from Mount Diablo* is a remarkable achievement. Its knowledge of the island, the entwining of private lives and politics, lifts Jamaican poetry to a level that has not been attempted before. The poetry is strong, imaginative, fascinating in detail. It describes terrible things with understatement, yet with compassion. ... Not only Jamaicans, but I think readers in England and the USA, will appreciate this book. It is something new.'

ISBN: 1-900715-81-3
Pages: 64
Published: 28 February 2003
Price: £7.99

Peepal Tree Press publishes a wide selection of outstanding fiction, poetry, drama, history and literary criticism with a focus on the Caribbean, Africa, the South Asian diaspora and Black life in Britain. Peepal Tree is now the largest independent publisher of Caribbean writing in the world. All our books are high quality original paperbacks designed to stand the test of time and repeated readings.

All Peepal Tree books should be available through your local bookseller, though you are even more welcome to place orders direct with us on the Peepal Tree website and on-line bookstore: www.peepaltreepress.com. You can also order direct by phone or in writing.

Peepal Tree sends out regular e-mail information about new books and special offers. We also produce a yearly catalogue which gives current prices in sterling, US and Canadian dollars and full details of all our books. Contact us to join our mailing list.

You can contact Peepal Tree at:

17 King's Avenue
Leeds LS6 1QS
United Kingdom

e-mail hannah@peepaltreepress.com
tel: 44 (0)113 245 1703

website: www.peepaltreepress.com